ACCIDENTAL GIFTS

A Castle Mountain Lodge Romance

ELENA AITKEN

Ink Blot Communications

Also by Elena Aitken

Castle Mountain Lodge

Unexpected Gifts

Hidden Gifts

Unexpected Endings - Short Story

Mistaken Gifts

Secret Gifts

Goodbye Gifts

Tempting Gifts

Holiday Gifts

Promised Gifts

Accidental Gifts

The Castle Mountain Lodge Collection: Books 1-3

The Castle Mountain Lodge Collection: Books 4-6

The Castle Mountain Lodge Collection: Books 7-9

The Castle Mountain Lodge Complete Collection

The Springs Series

Summer of Change

Falling Into Forever

Second Glances

Winter's Burn

Midnight Springs

She's Making A List

Summit of Desire

Summit of Seduction

Summit of Passion

Fighting For Forever

The Springs Collection: Volume 1

The Springs Collection: Volume 2

The Springs Collection: Volume 3

The Springs Complete Collection - Books 1-10

Destination Paradise

Shelter by the Sea

Escape to the Sun

Hidden in the Sand

Ever After

Choosing Happily Ever After

Needing Happily Ever After

Wanting Happily Ever After

Fighting Happily Ever After

We Wish You A Happily Ever After

Keeping Happily Ever After

Finding Happily Ever After

Seeking Happily Ever After

Cherishing Happily Ever After

Ever After: Volume One (Books 1-4)

The McCormicks

Love in the Moment

Only for a Moment

One more Moment

In this Moment

From this Moment

Our Perfect Moment

Stand Alone Stories

All We Never Knew

Drawing Free

Sugar Crash

Composing Myself

Betty & Veronica

The Escape Collection

Vegas

Nothing Stays in Vegas

Return to Vegas

Timber Creek

When We Left

When We Were Us

When We Began

When We Fell

Bears of Grizzly Ridge

His to Protect

His to Seduce

His to Claim

Hers to Take

His to Defend

His to Tame

His to Seek

Hers for the Season

Bears of Grizzly Ridge: Books 1-4

Bears of Grizzly Ridge: Books 5-8

Halfway Series

Halfway to Nowhere

Halfway in Between

Halfway to Christmas

Dear Reader,

Please note, Accidental Gifts was originally released as part of Melanie Shawn's Hope Falls Kindle World. I was honoured to write in Melanie's world and be part of that project.

The Kindle Worlds program has since been discontinued, and all references to Melanie Shawn's Hope Falls World have been removed from this version of the story. Accidental Gifts is no longer connected to Melanie's Shawn's amazing books.

I hope you enjoy your trip to Castle Mountain Lodge!

~Elena

To learn more about Melanie Shawn visit: www.melanieshawn.com

Chapter One

"TESS, you have to do it. It's not really a big deal and you'd really be helping me out."

Tess took her time swallowing the piece of muffin she'd been chewing before she answered her best friend. "No. I don't *have* to do it, it *is* a big deal and you're wrong, it would not be helping you out."

Clara had to be delusional if she thought that in any way Tess would be helping her out by impersonating her with an important client. And clearly she should seek medical attention, because her delusions could be symptoms of a more serious problem.

"It really would be helping me out. This is a no-brainer job anyway."

"Thanks."

If Clara caught the sarcasm, she didn't say anything.

"I've already taken care of all the hard work. All you have to do is take the client to Glacier Ridge Adventures and show them some of the options. It's super easy."

"He'll know I'm not you."

"No he won't," she said easily. "I've never met him. We've

only chatted on the phone a few times. Mostly we've been communicating via email anyway. Please do this. You owe me."

Tess most certainly did not owe Clara anything. At least, not that she could remember. Of course, there was the time when they were seventeen when Clara took the blame for the beers her dad found in her closet. And the time when Johnny Miller broke up with her when she'd been so sure he was going to ask her to marry him instead. Clara had dropped everything and come over, spending the whole weekend eating ice cream and drinking too much wine with her.

There were lots of times like that. But surely, none of those added up to a favor of this size.

"Clara. Even if I do owe you—" She held her finger up to silence the interruption before it began. "There is no way I can do this. You're the business consultant. Not me. I don't care how easy you *think* it is. I can't do it. I'm a payroll clerk, not a consultant. I don't know the first thing about business. I process paychecks."

"Correct me if I'm wrong." Her friend raised one eyebrow and took a sip of her drink. "But you're not processing any paychecks right now, are you? Including your own." Clara knew she had her on that point. Tess had been laid off from her job five weeks earlier and was having more than a little trouble finding a new one, which was why she'd agreed to accompany her friend out of Denver to the tiny town of Breckenridge for a work trip in the first place. What she had most decidedly *not* agreed on was impersonating her friend while she ran off with her current boy toy to Europe on a last-minute vacation.

"You know I'm not," she grumbled and took a long sip of her latte. "You don't need to point it out all the time."

Clara pulled a folder out of her bag and slapped it on the table. "I only point it out because this is your chance to actually *earn* a paycheck."

"What?"

"You don't think I'd ask you to do this for free, do you?"

If she were honest, Tess *had* expected to do it for free. She didn't need handouts from her best friend. She wasn't totally destitute. She had a savings account. Just like her dad had taught her when she got her first part-time job at sixteen. "Save for a rainy day, Tess. Always make sure you have at least three months' worth of your salary put away in case the unthinkable happens."

She hadn't listened to all her father's advice over the years, but she had listened to that little tidbit. Like a good girl, she dutifully saved and put away money. And she *definitely* had three months of salary put away. The only problem was, Tess took that advice when she was sixteen and working two days a week at Twisty Treat making ice cream cones. Turns out that even with ten years of interest, three months of salary from Twisty Treat a decade ago didn't add up to much. It certainly didn't add up to enough to live on for much longer than two months. If she didn't find some money, and soon, she wouldn't be able to pay rent. And she didn't even want to think about the balance on her credit card.

"How much money are we talking about?" Tess put her latte down and slowly slid the folder closer. It didn't mean she had to open it. But if it was closer…it wouldn't hurt to take a little peek…

"Normally I wouldn't do this," Clara said, "but because you'd really be helping me out with this one, I'll give you eighty percent of my fee."

"Eighty percent?" Tess would have liked to sound a lot more professional than she did, or at the very least, a little calmer. But it was hard to sound either professional *or* calm when choking on your coffee. She swallowed hard. "What type of money are we talking about?" Not that she'd turn anything down at that point, but it seemed like a logical question to ask.

She flipped the folder open and scanned through the contents. "And what exactly is *Glacier Ridge Adventures?*"

"It's this great place where they specialize in adventure activities. Just like the name suggests." Tess ignored her friend's sarcasm. "Zip-lining, horseback riding, kayaking— things like that. All you have to do is show him around and explain how he can integrate those types of activities into his existing business. I've done all the work for you. Just read my notes."

"No way." She slapped the folder shut. "Can't do it." That was putting it mildly. Tess simply did not *do* outdoor activities. Especially anything involving adventure of any kind. She was a city girl through and through. The very idea of going anywhere near a horse or a hike or anything at all that involved some sort of outdoor risk was definitely not her area of expertise. "You lost me at *outdoor.*"

"You're being ridiculous. Besides, you don't actually have to participate in any of the activities, just show him around. Meet with him a few times and go over the information I put in the file. Convince him how easy it would be to incorporate the same things with his business and detail the pros and cons. It's all right there." Clara pointed to the file again before she flipped through a few pages to a contract. "Including my fee," she added. "Remember. You'll get eighty percent."

Tess's eyes trailed down the page to where her friend was pointing and immediately widened. "Eighty percent? You're sure?"

Clara nodded.

Tess swallowed hard. *Decision made.* She was pretty sure she could put up with some dirt and a few bugs if it meant paying her rent for the next few months and maybe even taking care of some of that pesky credit card balance.

"So, you're in? Because I think I saw his car pull up."

"What?" Tess managed to pull her gaze away from the contract long enough to glare at her best friend. "Now?"

Clara's smile was sweet. "Yes. Remember, you're Clara Clark. Everything you need to know is in here and the client's name is Maxwell Grant. Here he comes."

With one final death stare at Clara, Tess turned around in her chair just in time to watch the sexiest man she'd ever laid eyes on walk through the door.

———

It had already been a long day. After a flight to Denver, followed by a two hour drive to the ski town of Breckenridge, the last thing Max wanted to do was have a meeting inside. He'd much rather tie his hiking boots on and hit the trails. For the last few hours, the scenery of the Colorado mountains had been tempting him and he was itching to get outside and explore.

It had been less than twenty-four hours since he'd been at Castle Mountain Lodge, surrounded by the Canadian Rockies. But the rocky peaks looked different in Colorado, and as nice as the town of Breckenridge seemed, he missed being outdoors. With any luck, the initial meeting with the consultant wouldn't take terribly long and he could go exploring.

There weren't many people in the little coffee shop, and his eyes immediately locked on a table with two women. Two very beautiful women. Maybe he could tolerate being inside for a little while longer. The blonde smiled broadly in his direction. She had to be Clara Clark.

"Hi there." He extended his hand. "You must be—"

"I'm Tess," she interrupted. "This is Clara. You must be Maxwell Grant, her client."

"Max." He tilted his head and looked at the brunette, who still sat quietly. She seemed to undergo some sort of transformation while he watched and must have remembered why she was there. Her pretty mouth turned up into a smile that didn't quite reach her eyes and she stood awkwardly.

"Sorry about that," she said. "I'm usually a little more prepared." She glanced quickly at her friend. "Why don't we all get some fresh coffee and get to know each other?"

"Oh no," Tess said. "I have to get going and the two of you probably have a lot of work to do. I wouldn't want to get in the way. Besides, I have to get going. After all, I do have a flight to catch."

"That's too—"

"I think you have time," Clara interrupted him and focused on her friend. "Your flight is a *charter* and besides, I thought you weren't leaving for a while yet. Stay and have a coffee." She gritted her teeth and gestured with her head to the table.

"Oh, I would if I could." The blonde stood from the table and gathered her purse. "But I'm sure you both have important work to do. So I'll go. Besides, there's a car waiting for me outside." She blew them both a kiss.

"A car?"

Max took a step back and watched the exchange between the two friends with a shake of a head. He might be an expert outdoorsman who'd come a little too close to a grizzly once or twice, scaled sheer rock faces, and rafted some of the worlds wildest rapids, but women were one thing he didn't think he'd ever get a handle on.

"Must run, darlin'. I'll touch base with you later this week."

And just like that, the bubbly blonde was gone and Clara looked stricken.

"Are you okay?" Max pulled a chair over and guided her to sit down again. "You look a little pale. Let me get you some water."

"Oh no. I'm—" She put her hand on his arm and the touch immediately sent a shock through him. Her too, obviously, as she stumbled over her next words. "I'm okay. I mean…I'm fine. I was just…never mind." She yanked her hand away and opened the file. "We should probably get to work."

Work was the last thing on Max's mind, especially after that touch. But it was the responsible thing to do. After all, the management of Castle Mountain Lodge had hired him to do a job and they were footing the bill for his trip to Breckenridge in an effort for him to collect as much information as he could about opening up an adventure park. For an outdoorsman like him, it was the perfect job. And he wasn't going to screw it up.

"I think that's a good idea, Clara." He pulled out a chair and sat across from her, trying not to focus on how pretty she was and how she didn't look anything at all like he'd pictured. She was softer somehow than the ambitious, no-nonsense tone of her emails. But then again, a lot could get lost in translation through email. Including the chemistry that obviously sizzled between them.

Chapter Two

THIS WAS CRAZY. The whole idea was absolutely insane. There was no way she could possibly pretend to be a consultant for an outdoor adventure park. Why couldn't it have been a coffee shop? Or a spa? Or even...anything at all.

They made small talk for a few minutes and Tess was careful to steer the conversation away from the actual reason they were there in order to buy herself a bit more time. Finally, she suggested that Max get himself a coffee so they could get down to business. The moment he got up, she flipped open the file and scanned it for any detail she could use.

Clara was right; everything she would need to know was in the file. The only problem was she didn't have time to read the file. Her eyes trailed down the first page until it landed on something she could use to get started: a list of the activities Glacier Ridge Adventures offered and a ranking system of how it would apply to Max's operation. Okay. She could work with that.

Feeling slightly more prepared—although only very slightly —she pulled that paper to the top of the pile and took a deep breath. She had a moment to watch him while he added sugar and cream to his drink. And was he ever something to watch.

Clearly he'd spent a great deal of time outdoors. His wide, strong shoulders were carved from hours likely spent chopping wood or climbing rocks, not that she could imagine anyone actually climbing rocks. But it seemed like something this man would do. Plus, it seemed like a very sexy thing to do. Not that Tess wanted anything to do with it. Not unless it meant looking at the muscles in Max's back. She could probably handle—

"Clara?"

She shook her head to snap herself out of her daydream in time to focus on the man in front of her—the real live object of her fantasy. "Sorry, what?" It was the stupidest thing she could have said, and the moment it came out of her mouth, she wished she could take it back.

His mouth turned up in a slow, sexy smile. "I just asked if I could get you anything." He put his cup on the table, but only slid into his seat when she shook her head no. The last thing Tess needed was more caffeine. If she was going to be able to get the job done, she was going to need to focus. And the sooner she got it done, the sooner she could cash the check and relax, knowing her bills were paid for at least another month or two.

"I guess we should get started." Tess hoped she sounded more confident than she felt. She certainly didn't have any experience in the subject, and acting had never been her strong suit—at least, that's what her high school drama teacher would say. But, there was no other choice. She'd just have to fake it. She opened the file and pulled out the piece of paper she'd decided to focus on. "From what I see here…I mean, what I've found…" The slip was fast and she covered it quickly, but she didn't miss the look of question in Max's eyes.

Shoot.

She smiled sweetly and kept going. "If your lodge is looking to integrate some more exciting activities, there are definitely some viable options that, from what I can see, should have an excellent rate of return. Are you ready to explore some of those?"

"I've never been more ready."

It was a cheesy thing to say, but coming out of Max's lips, it was one of the sexiest things she'd ever heard. It didn't hurt that Max simply oozed sexuality. Not that she needed to be thinking of him like that. She didn't need to be thinking of any man like that. With everything else she needed to be concerned about, men were definitely not making the list any time soon.

"Okay…" Tess clicked her pen a few times and scanned the list. "Zip-lining." She settled on the first thing she saw.

"What about it?" He grinned and took a sip of his coffee.

"Based on my research, zip-lining seems like an activity you should be able to integrate into Castle Mountain Lodge."

"Really?"

The way he questioned her made Tess second-guess herself. "Um…" She scanned the sheet again. "Yes." She swallowed hard and tried for way more confidence than she felt. "Based on my research and analysis, zip-lining as an activity for Castle Mountain Lodge scores a solid eight, making it an excellent choice. Glacier Ridge Adventures has experienced a lot of luck with it, and…" Tess called upon some information she remembered seeing on the Internet awhile back. "It seems to be very popular with both families and couples looking for a little adventure. A great choice."

Max tapped his pen against his lip. "Interesting. I would have thought the cost to install such an activity might affect the relevancy score. A mountain lodge in the Canadian Rockies isn't always the easiest place to build things like that. But if you say so…it's definitely worth a look. That's for sure."

She hadn't thought of the cost to install a zip line, but he absolutely had a point. What was Clara thinking? She took another look at the piece of paper in front of her. Kayaking scored a three. That didn't make any sense. Not that she knew much about kayaking either, but it seemed like a much easier activity to implement. Why would it score a lower mark?

Tess answered her own question when her eyes traveled to the top of the page and the legend of explanation that clearly laid out how the scoring system worked. The lower the score, the more relevant the activity. The higher the score, the less relevant it would be.

Crap.

Tess flipped the folder shut again before Max looked down and saw her screw-up for himself. "You know what else might be a good choice?" She smiled as sweetly as she could. *Blind him with bullshit, Tess.* "Kayaking."

"Kayaking?" Max leaned back in his chair and grinned. It was the type of grin that, if she wasn't so consumed by not utterly making a fool of herself, probably would have made her stomach flip and a silly girlish giggle come out of her. As it was, she couldn't let herself get distracted by anything else.

"Yes, kayaking. In fact, I think it's actually a much better choice. I just wanted to see if you were paying attention with the whole zip line thing." She hoped she sounded a whole lot more confident than she felt. "Let's talk about that."

"Kayaking sounds interesting, too," Max said. "But let's not totally abandon the idea of zip-lining yet."

"No?"

"No." He abruptly sat up and placed his hands on the table. "In fact, I think we should go out to Glacier Ridge right now and check it out."

Something that was way too close to panic filled Tess at the very idea of going anywhere near a zip line. "I don't know if that's necessary. Sometimes talking it through is the best course of action. Why don't we—"

"Come on." Max hopped up from his chair and held out a

hand to her. "I insist. It's really best to get out there and experience these things first hand. Besides, I'm the client and isn't there a saying that goes something like 'the client is always right'?"

For a second, Max actually felt a little bad when he saw the panic on Clara's face. Or whoever she really was. Because no matter what she said, the woman who'd been sitting in front of him for the last thirty minutes trying to sell him on adding crazy activities like zip-lining to Castle Mountain Lodge was most definitely not the Clara Clark he'd been corresponding with. In fact, the more he thought about it, there was a good chance that the blonde who'd been with her when he arrived was likely the woman he was supposed to be meeting with.

She was probably one of Clara's colleagues, although she really didn't seem to have a clue about his business. And although there wasn't anything overtly obvious, Max's instincts told him he was definitely not dealing with the same consultant he'd been working with via email.

He couldn't figure out who this woman was, and if she wasn't so damn cute, he might even be upset about it. But he wasn't. She obviously was trying to do a job she wasn't adequately prepared for and her heart seemed to be in the right place, so she wasn't really hurting anyone. Besides, the only reason he'd even agreed to hiring a consultant on this project was because the owners of the Lodge and the new general manager Melissa Kramer had insisted. They signed his paycheck, so who was he to argue?

He already knew what he wanted to do up at the Lodge to add an adventurous appeal, and it wasn't likely that anything the cute little brunette had to say would change his mind anyway. So, as far as he was concerned, there really was no harm in him playing along with her little game. In fact, he was pretty sure he could have a little fun with it. No, he could have *a lot* of fun with it.

"Are you ready?" he asked when she didn't immediately stand and take him up on his offer to go check out the zip line. "I mean, there's no time like the present."

She paused and her cute little mouth opened and closed before it finally pressed into a tight line.

"Of course," she said through gritted teeth and a smile so false Max had to work at not laughing out loud. If his suspicions were correct, there was a very good chance this woman had never even seen a zip line, let alone tried one.

This was going to be fun.

"We'll take my car." Once outside of the little Café, Max held his hand out and gently steered her in the direction of his rented SUV. He'd toyed with the idea of getting her to drive to the location she'd obviously never been to before, and as entertaining as it might have been to watch her squirm as she tried to continue this deception, ultimately Max's chivalrous nature won out. He'd never let a woman drive him around before, and he wasn't about to start now.

He opened the door for her and she slid inside. The second the door was shut, she dropped her head into her hands and shook it quickly when she obviously thought he wasn't watching. But he was. Oh, he most definitely *was* watching her. He couldn't not. Not only was she gorgeous, she was fascinating. And the prospect of seeing how far he could push her was definitely going to make his trip to Breckenridge a whole lot more interesting than he'd originally thought.

"I was just thinking." Clara spoke up after they'd been driving for a few minutes. "We probably had to make reservations for the zip line. It's a busy time of year and all." She wouldn't make eye contact with him, focusing instead on the papers in front of her. "There's a good chance we won't be able to check it out today. But that's okay. I mean, I'm sure a guy like you has had plenty of experience with stuff like that."

Max swallowed a smile. "What do you mean, a guy like me?"

"Oh, nothing." She laughed, a high-pitched nervous trill that he couldn't help but find ridiculously cute. "I just meant that you seem like a really outdoorsy type of guy who's probably been on a zip line before. You'd know what it's like. You wouldn't actually have to see this one."

"Oh yes." He nodded, working hard to keep his face a perfect mask of seriousness. "I definitely need to see this one. After all, my job here is to make sure that I'm bringing in the right type of activities to Castle Mountain Lodge and the only way I can do that is if I personally try each and every one of them. And I'm so lucky to have you with me because it'll be very important to not only get your professional opinion, *Clara Clark*"—he emphasized her name— "but also to get your first-hand experience with everything. My bosses will definitely be interested in getting the opinion of a woman. After all, Castle Mountain Lodge is largely visited by couples."

"Couples? Really?" Tess saw the opportunity to change the subject and jumped on it. She'd figure out how to get out of the zip line situation later. Because there was no way she was going anywhere near a contraption that would have her sailing through the air with the ground a hundred feet below her. No, thank you; she'd be keeping her feet firmly planted on the ground. "Tell me a bit more about the Lodge."

He glanced at her out of the corner of his eye. "Shouldn't you have all the information about the Lodge already? I'm pretty sure I sent you all of our promotional materials and of course there was our email correspondence."

"Oh, of course." Tess covered quickly. This deception thing was already way harder than she'd expected it to be. Not that she had any expectations at all. "But reading about something is not nearly as good as hearing about it firsthand. I'd like to hear your take on Castle Mountain Lodge. It sounds amazing. Tell me about it."

He nodded and focused his eyes back on the road that would presumably take them to Glacier Ridge Adventures. She could have kissed him when he offered to drive. It's not that she wasn't capable of typing an address into her GPS function on her phone, but she was pretty sure that Clara had been to the resort already a time or two, and she was supposed to at least give the illusion of knowing what she was talking about.

"It's amazing." Max started to talk, and much to her relief, as soon as he mentioned the woods and the mountains, he got lost in his explanations and Tess found herself getting caught up in his words. There was so much passion in the way he spoke about the Rocky Mountains and the Lodge he worked at. It seemed like so much more than just a place to work and she told him so.

"It is," he said in response. "The Lodge is way more than just a job, but I'm very fortunate to be able to live there and get paid to do what I love. That's not always the case when you choose a career like mine."

"And what exactly is that career?" She didn't mean for her words to sound snarky. Not in the least, but she also had a hard time understanding what it was exactly that Max Grant did. From what she could tell, he got paid to play outside all day. Not that it sounded like her kind of play. Not at all. It wasn't that she hated the outdoors: Tess enjoyed a nice walk in the park on a sunny day as much as the next person. It was the forest and anything beyond city limits that tended to scare the crap out of her.

If Max was offended by her question, he didn't show it.

"My official title is adventure activity manager. I know it's hard to understand and even some days I have to pinch myself to remind myself that I'm lucky enough to have this life. Basically, my job with the Lodge is to bring adventure to their offerings for guests. They have an outdoor activities manager. Bo Clancy. He's a great guy and he's great at what he does, but I'm the guy to bring in the really good stuff."

"Being the zip line?" Even saying the word made Tess's insides shake.

"Exactly. If it's practical." He winked at her. "And some other activities as well. After all, you have the list."

"Of course." She smiled as professionally as she could manage. "I'll be able to guide you with all the right decisions about what activities you need to bring to the Lodge." She couldn't be certain, but she was pretty sure she saw Max roll his eyes.

Whatever. She was there to do a job and that's exactly what she was going to do. If she could just survive the next few hours. She had the distinct impression that Max was going to expect her to try the activities and there was no way in hell that Tess Rogers was going anywhere near a zip line.

But Clara Clark would.

Damn. She was going to kill her friend.

As if Clara could tell from a distance that Tess was cursing her under her breath, her phone chirped with an incoming text message.

How's it going?

Tess smiled over at Max. "It's just my girlfriend from earlier. Excuse me for a second."

I'm going to kill you, she typed back.

Sounds like it's going well. Just follow the plan in the folder.

What plan? She hadn't seen any *plan.* Just some sheets full of information and specs. And that silly rating system that had already gotten her into trouble once. There was certainly no *plan.*

What plan?

"Is everything okay?" Max asked.

She glanced in his direction in time to see his smirk before he focused his eyes back on the road. Either he was very cocky or he knew she was a fake. It had to be the former. There was no way he'd have any reason to think she was anything but an ill-prepared consultant. She definitely wasn't perfect, but she'd done a pretty damn good job of fibbing so far. At least she thought she had.

"Of course," she said smoothly, tucking her phone away. It wasn't as though Clara was going to be any actual help anyway.

"Good. Because we're here."

Chapter Three

MAX PULLED the SUV into the parking lot in front of the main building of Glacier Ridge Adventures and cut the engine. "Are you ready for this?" He felt a twinge of guilt at the pleasure he was taking from seeing her squirm, but just a twinge. After all, it was clearly her who was doing the deceiving and it's not as if he was causing any actual harm.

She nodded. With a smile so fake he almost gave in, she said, "Of course. It's not as if it's my first time." Her confidence, even if she was forcing it, was definitely attractive. *Very* attractive. "But like I said, I'm not sure they'll be able to fit us in on such short notice. After all, there are a few cars here and they probably have scheduled tours already booked. I'm not sure that we——"

"We won't know if we don't try, will we?"

She swallowed hard, and for a second Max was pretty sure she was going to come clean and out herself. To his surprise, she didn't. Instead, she gathered up her bag, shoved the folder inside and clutched it to her chest. "Okay, let's go see what we can see."

He shook his head with a little smile as he followed her up

the path to the main office. Whoever she was, she was certainly cute. If you liked the city girl type. And to his surprise, he did. He watched her navigate the gravel path with her high heels and let his gaze slide up her legs. He took his time drinking in her curves showcased in her form-fitting jeans. It was most definitely a sight he could watch all day.

If it wasn't for the step.

"Dammit." Max cursed under his breath as he tried without much success to shake off the pain radiating through the foot he'd just stubbed into the step he hadn't seen. Because he'd been watching his way too attractive companion.

Who was now looking at him with a satisfied grin on her face. "You okay?"

He nodded.

"If you're sure," she said. "Because I'd understand if you—"

"We're going zip-lining." Max stepped purposely on his now throbbing foot and took the steps two at a time to join her by the door, which he opened in a flourish. "Shall we?"

She walked confidently into the building and straight to the desk. "Excuse me," she said to the girl behind the desk. "My name is Clara Clark and this is Max Grant. I've been emailing with Sarah Gibbons about some of her operations and I was wondering if she was available to speak with."

"It's fine if she isn't," Max jumped in. "Because what we really want to do is check out the zip line."

"But we really should spend some time speaking with Sarah."

He didn't miss the glare she shot his way. She really didn't want to get anywhere near the zip line. Her stalling techniques were impressive to be sure, but Max wasn't the type of guy to be swayed when he wanted something. And he definitely wanted something.

"I'm sure we can see her another time."

"They probably don't have any space for us to——"

"Are you two almost finished?" The girl behind the desk interrupted their banter. "Because if you want to talk to me, I have a few minutes right now, but then I have to run into a meeting and then I'd be more than happy to send you with my partner Blake to check out the zip line."

Both of them turned their attention to the girl who'd more or less outed herself as Sarah Gibbons, the owner of Glacier Ridge Adventures. Max couldn't be sure which one of them was more surprised, but he certainly wasn't the first to recover.

"Sarah." Clara held out her hand. "It's so nice to meet you in person. I'm so sorry that I didn't let you know ahead of time that we'd be coming."

"But you did," Sarah said. "In your email last week, you mentioned that you'd be meeting with Max and he'd probably want to try out some of our activities."

"I did?"

Max raised an eyebrow. "You did?"

"Of course I did." In a flash, the frown was gone from her face, replaced by the sweet smile Max was already growing very fond of. "I don't know where my head is today. It's been a very strange afternoon and I'm just not myself. You have a few minutes to talk then?"

"I do." Sarah looked strangely between the two of them. "But quite honestly, I'm not really sure what more I can tell you than what I've already told you. I think your time might be better spent trying things out for yourself. Come on, I'll go grab Blake for you."

———

Max almost felt bad for his *advisor* as they were shuffled into a Jeep to be driven to the staging area, where they were given harnesses, helmets, and a thorough safety speech before they were led to the first platform. She'd put on a brave face while Blake snugged her into her harness, and Max couldn't help but feel a twinge of jealousy at the close contact the other man had with her. It was completely ridiculous considering they hadn't even known each other a full twenty-four hours, and hell, he still didn't even know her real name.

You could ask. A little voice, the voice of reason that should be telling him to quit the game and just come clean that he knew she wasn't Clara Clark, spoke up for at least the tenth time since they'd gotten in the car together. But he couldn't do it. Not yet. It had been way too long since he'd had a little fun. And messing with the pretty little brunette was just the little bit of fun he needed. Besides, he wasn't hurting anybody. Not really. He was the one who was being messed with. So at least for the time being, he planned to enjoy every minute he had with *Clara.*

"This is going to be amazing," he said when Blake finished explaining the first zip line. The course was made up of more than one line; the first one was definitely not the longest, but there was always something thrilling about that first time stepping off the platform and letting your body fly through the air. "You should go first."

"Oh no." She shook her head and took a step backward but ran into the railing. Her hands shot out on each side and her fingers gripped the wooden rails. Max could see the white of her knuckles and he had another shot of remorse for what he was doing. But she was just the type of woman who *needed* to try a zip line. He knew her type. Repressed city girls who spent their entire lives making safe decisions and making sure they were firmly in control of everything in their lives at all times... they were the ones who needed zip lines the most. She'd thank him for it later.

"Come on, *Clara.*" He emphasized her name.

"It'll be fine." Blake stepped forward and gently led Clara

to the platform. "Bruce is on the other side and he'll catch you. All you have to do is step off. Put your legs straight out in front of you; put your right hand here." He placed her hand on the clip he'd just fastened while he spoke. "And enjoy the ride. You'll never experience anything quite like it. Are you ready?"

To Max's surprise, she nodded. Before she could change her mind, Blake gave her a little push and she stepped off the platform.

———

Oh my God. Oh my God. Oh my God.

Those were the only three words repeating in Tess's head as she hurtled through the air at a zillion miles an hour. But the only sound coming out of her mouth was a blood-curdling scream. Her eyes were squeezed so tight they stung but after a moment, when she realized she was neither dead, nor did she think she was going to die in the immediate future, Tess slowly opened one eye.

Time both seemed to slow down and speed up as the world hurtled past her in a blur of trees. To her total surprise and delight, she opened both eyes then to take in the incredible sight. And it *was* incredible. Never in her life had Tess seen anything like the view she had from the treetops.

And then it was over.

Her feet, in the sneakers borrowed from Sarah, made contact with the platform, and Bruce expertly slowed her. "Put your feet down," he instructed.

She did and just like that, her trip through the air was over.

"That's it?"

"That's it. You did great. How was it?"

"It was the most amazing thing I've ever done! I can't believe it went so fast. The trees—they were...the air...it was...up so high...incredible."

Bruce laughed. "I'm glad you liked it." He quickly unclipped her harness and led her up to the other side of the platform. "Stand here and you can watch your friend come in. He should be taking off in three…two…here he comes."

She could only barely see Max's dark form as he began his trek, but could she ever hear him. He wasn't screaming the way she had, but instead was making a noise that could only be described as Goofy's laugh as he flew toward her. And then he was there, expertly landing on the platform, with very little assistance from Bruce. When he was unclipped, he turned immediately to find her.

"What did you think?" He joined her where she stood, still in awe as to what she'd just done. "Never mind. I can tell that you loved it."

She couldn't even bother to pretend she hadn't. A smile split her face. "It was incredible. I've never experienced anything like it. It was as if…I don't…"

"As if you came alive for the first time?"

"Yes!" She grabbed his arm and squeezed. "That's it exactly. You have to put a zip line in at Castle Mountain. You *have* to. For your guests to experience something like that. For them to come alive like that. Like I did…you have to."

Max laughed and if she hadn't been so preoccupied with the euphoria running through her, she might have noticed how incredibly good-looking he was when he laughed. At least, she would have noticed a little bit more than she already did. "So now you think it's a good idea? I thought you were just *testing* me." He held up his hands and made air quotes.

Dammit. She'd forgotten about that.

Tess shook her head and made a split-second decision. One Clara would probably kill her for. But she didn't care. Clara had a lot of explaining to do on her own. She'd deal with her later. "I've changed my mind," she announced. "Based on firsthand experience, I think you absolutely should put a zip line in. After all, I'm the expert, right?"

He shook his head and laughed. "That you are."

A moment later, Blake zipped through the air and landed on the platform next to them. "By the smiles on your faces, I'd say you enjoyed that. Ready for more?"

Never in a million years did Tess think she would find herself nodding eagerly and jumping to be the first in line. But that's exactly what she did for the rest of the course. When they were finished, they joined Blake and Sarah for a quick chat and a tour around the rest of the grounds. Spending time with the couple, who were both equally enthusiastic about their business and the activities that they offered, was exactly what Tess needed. Both to come down from the excitement of the day and to let someone else do most of the talking. Max peppered them with questions and Tess dutifully scribbled notes and made a list of questions to ask Clara when she could finally get her friend on the phone. This acting job was turning out to be a great deal harder than she'd expected. Max turned to see her watching him and he gave her a smile that made her melt like a chocolate bar on a summer's day. *But it was worth it.*

The thought popped into her head out of nowhere but she didn't bother to push it away, because it *was* definitely worth it.

By the time they got back in the car and Max pulled out of the parking lot to head back into town, he had a decidedly different attitude. He snuck a glance over at the woman who'd done nothing but surprise him all day. The hair that had been so perfect earlier in the day was now tousled with a sexy look, very reminiscent of a woman who'd just had a romp in bed. The thought shot a spark through him, directly to his core. Damn. He had no business thinking of this woman in any way but a professional one. But then again, she obviously wasn't the woman he hired, so really it didn't cross any lines or break any rules if he wanted to think of her any way at all. And much to Max's surprise, he did want to think about her.

In fact, he wanted to think about her a lot. He'd experienced all of the activities that they'd just participated in. He'd zip-lined, he'd climbed through ropes courses; heck, he'd climbed entire mountains before. But doing it with her was as if he'd done everything for the first time. Sure, Max had expected to have a little fun with her, pushing her and teasing her. But he'd never actually expected to really *enjoy* himself. And he had.

More than that, he really didn't want the day to end.

"So, I guess you have enough now to make a decision?" Her question broke his train of thought and the daydream he was having about extending their little meeting. Possibly into the evening. "Max?" she prompted when he didn't answer right away. "Are you ready to make a decision?"

He needed to answer her. But he didn't need to give her the truth—that long before she'd even met with him, he had his answer. She was waiting for him to say something, but all he could think about was how to keep her there with him a little bit longer.

"No," he said before he realized the word had come out of his mouth. "But I'm getting closer. There's one thing I really think we should do before I make up my mind."

Her brow wrinkled up in question. "We already went through my entire report, went on the zip line, climbed the ropes…what else could you possibly need to make a final decision?"

"We'll need to go to the Lodge." The second the idea popped into his head, he spoke it out loud without thinking it through. But he didn't need to. It was a brilliant idea. "Yes," he said, confirming his idea. "I need you to visit Castle Mountain

Lodge and see the site for yourself so you can help me make the best decision."

He was spouting a pile of nonsense, but if she noticed, she didn't show it. Instead, worry and confusion lined her face. "I don't know, Max. I mean, isn't that outside the scope of what I'm supposed to be doing?"

"Nonsense. We hired you to do a job, and I think the only way you can make an informed decision is to actually see the Lodge. Don't you?"

"Umm…" She pulled out her phone and frantically tapped. "I just need to send a text. Can you give me a second?"

Of course she did. He'd forgotten for a brief second that she wasn't who she said she was. She'd need to check with whoever was really in charge of the little deception she was playing at. Possibly the real Clara Clark.

It only took a few minutes of frantic texting before she tucked her phone away and sighed. "Okay," she said. "I can go. I'll need a few days to make arrangements, though."

Max nodded. "Of course. I'll tell you what: I'll change my flight to stay an extra few days and I'll book you on the same flight." He pulled into the parking lot in front of the cafe, where they'd left her vehicle. "I can meet you at the airport on…Thursday? Does that give you enough time?"

"No!" Her pretty face contorted into a frown and for a minute he thought she might be sick. "I mean Thursday is fine but…I'll book the ticket. Just send me your flight information. I'll take care of it." She gathered her things, opened the door and was standing outside before Max even realized what had happened.

He rolled down the window and called to her as she practically sprinted across the parking lot to her car. "Clara." When she didn't answer, he called louder. "Clara!" She stopped and turned. "Thank you for today," he said. "I had fun."

The smile that crossed her face gave him that funny feeling in the pit of his stomach again.

"So did I," she said. "I'll see you Thursday."

It wasn't until he watched her drive away that Max realized she'd likely panicked about the flight because if he was in charge, she'd have to reveal her real name. No matter. He planned to get to the bottom of whatever game she was playing. And he was going to have even more fun doing it, too.

Because whatever her name was, one thing was certain: Max couldn't remember the last time he'd enjoyed himself so much. And he didn't plan to let that feeling get away so easily.

Chapter Four

THERE WASN'T enough wine to get her through this. But at the same time, there could definitely be too much wine. Two days after more or less running from Max's car in Breckenridge, Tess found herself sitting at the Denver airport, nursing a glass of white wine in the departures lounge. What she really wanted to do was drain the glass and order another one. She was going to need all the strength she could get to make it through more pretending to be Clara. Even if it was liquid courage.

As long as she didn't get drunk. She needed her wits about her to be sure. Especially considering she couldn't help but get the distinct impression from Max that he was testing her in some way. Almost as if he knew she had no idea what she was talking about. If she got fired—or really…got *Clara* fired from that job—that would mean no commission and no rent money. No. It wasn't an option. She needed to pull it together. But one more sip couldn't hurt.

She had just lifted the glass to her lips when the deep voice she'd actually dreamed about came from behind her. She couldn't react fast enough and Tess sort of half choked and half spat out the mouthful of wine. She didn't need a mirror to tell her that her face was likely the same shade of bright red as her carry-on suitcase.

"Are you okay?"

Max slid his hand between her shoulder blades and gave her back a small rub that sent shock waves of something that was way too close to desire through her body.

"I'm fine." Tess gave him what she hoped was a convincing smile as he took the seat next to her. "I probably shouldn't be drinking anyway. After all, it is a business trip." The thought just occurred to her. "I'm so sorry. It's terribly inappropriate of me to—"

"Wine is a little inappropriate." His face was stern and Tess held her breath, hoping he wouldn't fire her on the spot. Which was ridiculous, because besides feeling insecure about her terrible acting skills, she'd really not given him any reason at all to fire her. "We're heading to the Canadian Rockies." He waved his hand to catch the bartender's eye. "You should be having beer." He grinned at her and in that instant, all her reservations about taking the trip were gone. "I'll have a pint of Canadian."

The beer appeared and Max paid both bills before he turned to face her. "Are you ready for this?"

"For the trip?" She nodded and reached into her bag to pull out the file that she'd more or less memorized since their last meeting. Tess felt much more prepared, and after a few phone calls with Clara, had some solid points to discuss with Max. "I am." She started to open the file. "I have a few more ideas that—"

His warm, much larger hand covered hers, forcing her to close the file before she could open it completely. "No," he said. "No business."

"But that's why we're going." She couldn't take her eyes off his hand, which hadn't moved from hers.

"No." Her eyes flew up. "I mean, yes," Max quickly. "But I hope that's not the only reason for the trip."

What the heck did he mean by that? Of course it was the only reason for the trip. There was no way she'd voluntarily get on a plane to fly to Canada with a strange man if it wasn't for business. Unless, of course, the man had dark eyes that were currently piercing her with an intensity that was doing all kinds of crazy things to her insides.

No. Eyes or not, she would never take a trip like this if it wasn't out of need.

When Tess didn't answer right away, Max continued, "Have you been to Canada before?" She shook her head. She'd never had the opportunity to travel north. Or anywhere, really. "It's the most beautiful country. Especially where the Lodge is. The mountains are…well, they're just something else. It's almost magical. Hard to explain, really." His eyes glossed over as he lost himself in the memory, and then it was gone and he put a bright smile back on his face as he took a deep drink of his beer. "But you'll see for yourself soon enough. I think we're almost ready to board." He tipped his drink up and finished the beer he'd just barely started. Tess took one more sip of her wine and decided it was better if she left it unfinished.

"I'm ready," she lied.

The truth was, she didn't think she'd ever be ready for spending the next few days pretending to be someone she wasn't, doing something she had no idea how to do, as if her future depended on her doing the job well. Which it did. As if that wasn't bad enough, she had to maintain her composure in close proximity to a ridiculously sexy mountain man who happened to have been the star of all her dreams—both sleeping and waking—for the last few days.

Max grabbed her bag away from her, the perfect gentleman, and Tess sent a silent prayer up. She couldn't remember the last time she'd called on a higher power, but if the last few minutes was any indication, she was going to need all the help she could get.

Tess Rogers.

Tess.

That was her name.

It was like a little secret, and the moment he'd seen the name printed on her passport as she handed it to the airline attendant before she boarded, he almost wished he hadn't. No, that wasn't true. He *was* glad he knew. It was a beautiful name and it suited her perfectly. But it did make it harder to continue his role in the little game they were playing. The truth was, he didn't care whether she was Clara Clark or Tess Rogers, or Julia Roberts. And he really didn't care whether she had anything to say about adventure activities at Castle Mountain Lodge. All he cared about was spending more time with her.

It was all he'd thought about since he'd watched her walk away two days earlier. Clara—no, *Tess*—had been the star of every waking thought and every sleeping thought, too. He couldn't remember the last time he had a woman take over his thoughts so completely. Probably because it had never happened before.

And it shouldn't be happening now.

There was nothing about Tess Rogers that he should be attracted to.

Except her long, soft hair, her curves that just begged to be touched, her crystal-clear blue eyes and those lips that curled up into the most delicious smile. There was all that.

But there was also the stylish, likely overpriced clothes, the heels so high they'd snap off the second she stepped onto a trail, and the perfectly manicured hands that he could guarantee had never held an oar. She was a city girl through and through, and he was a self-declared mountain man. He thrived in the woods. He needed to be on a trail, surrounded by trees and high peaks. Give him a river to cast into over a big box grocery store any day. They were total opposites. Never mind the fact that he wasn't even supposed to know who she was.

That was a little detail he focused on during the four-hour flight. Of course he'd suspected she was playing games with him, but suspecting and knowing was different. He should have been upset with her for playing him a fool. And he probably would have been if he hadn't been so completely taken with her.

Max had done little more than think about the perfectly polished city girl and the wild look in her eyes after she'd flown across her first zip line. No. Wild wasn't even the word to describe it. It was more like *freedom*. In that moment, Tess had looked completely free, as if she had been holding back her entire life and he'd been the one to bring it out in her.

He liked that idea. A lot. It didn't matter one bit that she was lying to him. Okay…it mattered a little.

By the time they landed and made their way through the airport to his truck, Max had made a decision. He wanted to get to know her, despite her secrets. Maybe because of them. Either way, it didn't matter. There was something about her. Besides, surely after a few days together, she'd come clean with the truth. She'd have to.

"It's beautiful here."

"June is one of my favorite months in the mountains," Max

said. "The chill of the spring has gone away, but it's still not quite summer."

Tess had been mostly quiet on their journey, choosing to immerse herself in the information she'd researched on mountain lodges, Castle Mountain Lodge specifically, before falling asleep on the plane. Once they got into Max's truck, he'd kept up a steady stream of chatter as they drove, leaving the city behind, and made their way closer to the mountains. But once their travels finally brought them into the Rocky Mountains, Tess could no longer bite her tongue. She'd never seen anything quite as spectacular as the stone peaks that rose up all around her. She'd grown up in Colorado around mountains, but these were different. A little higher, a little more…rugged and wild.

She craned her head around, trying to get a better look through the windshield. "They go on forever!"

"They sure look like it." Max chuckled. "But I can tell you from firsthand experience, they don't. I've stood on the top of that one."

"What?" Tess whipped around to stare at him. "You did what?" She turned back in the direction he pointed. "That one?"

"That's the one. Mount Athabasca. It's actually a pretty basic hike most of the way. Once you get to altitude, there's some scrambling and real climbing though. We could go if you want?"

"What?" Tess shook her head. "No. I don't think so."

"You don't hike?" His eyes were teasing, but his question was serious. "At all?"

"Well…" She looked out the window again. "No. Not really." And by *not really* she meant *not at all*. Not unless you counted a long walk through a city park, but she was pretty sure Max wouldn't.

"I can't believe that," he said. "Okay, actually I can."

"Pardon?" She glared at him. "What is that supposed to mean?"

"Just that you don't really seem like the hiking type. I mean, no offense, but you don't seem like the outdoor type at all. I'm surprised, actually."

"How so?"

"Your bio."

Bio. Tess racked her brain. *What bio?*

"On your website," he continued. "It said something about Clara Clark spending as much time outdoors as she could. Blah blah blah. Hiking through rain forests, camping on beaches."

Oh shit. Of course. Clara's bio read like something out of an adventure magazine. Primarily because she only dated men who would whisk her to exotic locations around the globe and do crazy things like that with her. It made sense that Max would have done his research on her. Or Clara. She shook her head. It was a good thing there were no head shot pictures of Clara on her website. She'd chosen for more of a "lifestyle" approach. Which meant there were only shots of her hiking and skiing and...doing the very things Tess had just admitted she'd never done.

Shoot.

She had to think quickly because something told her Max would not take kindly to knowing he'd been totally duped by an out of work payroll clerk, instead of the professional he'd hired. "Oh, that." She waved her hand and tried for a super casual tone. "I probably shouldn't tell you this, but those website bios are all propaganda. I mean, don't hold it against me or anything, but..." She leaned in for effect and was almost thrown off her story by the scent of him. All raw, masculine and...*damn.* Tess took a deep breath to steady herself, but it backfired as her senses filled with the scent that was pure Max. She leaned back and with some concentrated effort, finished what she was trying to say. "It's all made up to appeal to a wider audience." She barely managed to get the words out. *How was it even possible for one man to smell so freakin' good?*

"Is that right?" His mouth twisted up into a sly grin, and for a second, Tess was pretty sure she was going to get called out. Instead, he said, "Well then, I think it's time you quit lying."

"What?"

Maybe she *was* going to get called out. A trail of cold sweat beaded along her spine.

Crap. Crap. Crap.

How the hell was she going to get out of this? If he called her out on lying to him, it was over. Clara would kill her and worse, she wouldn't get paid and she'd lose her apartment. *And him.*

That thought came out of nowhere. She didn't *have* him, so she couldn't possibly lose him. But she could lose the time she was spending with him, which to her surprise, she was enjoying more and more.

It was almost worth the stress of the whole thing.

"I'm not lying," she finally managed to squeak the words out.

"You are too—you just said so." His smile told her he knew a lot more than he was saying, but to her relief, all he said was, "About your bio."

The bio. Right.

"Why would you say all those things in your bio if you didn't mean them? And more to the point, why not actually start to experience those things so you aren't lying anymore?"

"Wait. What?"

He wasn't busting her. He was just calling her to task.

"I mean, you can change your bio," he continued. "Or... I'll just spend the next few days helping you cross off some of those things off your list. How does that sound?"

Terrible was how it sounded. The very idea of Tess trying to be even half as adventurous as Clara was terrified her. But then when she looked at Max, she couldn't help it. He was so assured, so confident, and so damn sexy. "I think it sounds good," she said before she even knew the words had come out of her mouth. "Let's do it."

Chapter Five

MAX CERTAINLY HADN'T THOUGHT she would agree so easily. What he'd really expected was for her to come clean about who she was and then they could actually begin the process of getting to know each other and possibly...*no*. He couldn't think about what would come after they got to know each other. Because really, what was that? Sex? A relationship?

The very thought of the word almost caused him to laugh out loud. He'd never had a relationship, but it wasn't because of the reasons most people would suspect. It wasn't because he was a loner, a wanderer who never wanted to settle down. Not at all. He'd never had an actual relationship because he'd never had that feeling before. The feeling that he couldn't live one day without seeing a woman. That feeling in the pit of his stomach that told him *she* was the one.

Max had never had any of that. And when he did, he'd know it was right and he'd do anything to make it real.

"We're almost there." He pointed out the window as he turned the truck onto the side road that would take them up to Castle Mountain Lodge. "If you look out your window, you'll see the sign soon."

She shook her head. "I still can't believe I'm here. This is absolutely beautiful. I mean, Breckenridge is pretty, but…"

"There's nothing quite like the Canadian Rockies," he finished for her. "I've traveled all over this world, and there definitely are some amazing places out there, but there's no place like—"

"Home?"

Max laughed. "It's home for now, I guess. And I plan to enjoy every moment of it." He glanced at her and held her gaze for a moment. He also planned to enjoy every moment with her.

"Oh. I see it."

Max turned his focus back to the road as they passed the large wooden sign announcing their arrival. He knew it would only be a moment before the Lodge came into view. And then—

"Oh my goodness." Tess practically bounced in her seat. "It's…it's absolutely spectacular."

A grin crossed his face, because it was spectacular. The main building of Castle Mountain Lodge was constructed of a mixture of huge logs and natural stone that almost melted into the surrounding mountains and forest. He parked the truck right out front of the oversized sliding glass doors. Almost immediately, Ryan Morrison, the guests service manager, greeted them and opened Tess's door for her. Max had let him know there were coming and told him he planned to give Tess the entire Castle Mountain experience.

"Welcome to Castle Mountain Lodge." Ryan held out his hand for Tess to take as she stepped down out of the truck.

"Thank you. It's absolutely amazing."

"Oh, you haven't seen anything yet." Max joined her next to the truck. "Wait until we go inside."

"I think you're going to enjoy your stay here. I'm Ryan, the guest services manager, and if there is anything I can do to make your stay more enjoyable, please don't hesitate to ask. Although, I'm pretty sure you're in good hands here with Max."

Tess laughed. It was a beautiful sound. "I'm Te—Clara Clark. Thank you so much for having me here on such short notice. I'm really looking forward to seeing the Lodge firsthand and seeing how we can help you implement some of the activities Max and I have already discussed."

He had to bite his lip to keep from laughing. She was trying so hard to maintain the role of business consultant. He really needed her to let it go. And he was hoping that the very first thing he had planned for her would do just that.

"She's in very good hands." Max handed Ryan the keys to his truck. "In fact, I have a full schedule planned for us, so we should get started."

"Absolutely." Ryan gave Max an envelope. "I've booked Ms. Clark into our second best room. My apologies, Clara, but our very best room is taken by some very special guests and friends of the Lodge, Gage Mitchell and his girlfriend, Megan Powers."

"Gage Mitchell? Really? Isn't he the star of…"

"*Tumbleweed*," Ryan finished for her. "Yes, he is. He and his girlfriend, Megan, try to come back to visit a few times a year. They actually met here and fell in love. The Lodge is kind of a special place for them. In fact, Castle Mountain Lodge is known for bringing people together. Lots of couples fall in love at the Lodge."

Ryan looked pointedly between Max and Tess, a look Max didn't miss. He'd heard the stories of all the people who'd come together at the Lodge; he just never thought he'd be one of them.

Until that moment.

Tess had only been at Castle Mountain Lodge for less than an hour and already she didn't want to leave. Ever.

It was amazing, but that wasn't even the best word to describe it. Not even close. It just didn't feel adequate to explain the feeling that had come over her the moment she'd stepped out of Max's truck.

Peaceful. Inspired. *Home.*

Tess shook her head and splashed water on her face. She needed to clear her mind. She was being ridiculous. After all, it was easy to feel at home in a spectacular condo suite with a mountain directly out her back floor-to-ceiling windows. When Ryan said it was their second best room, she had been prepared for a stunning room. But nothing could have prepared her for what she actually got. But it wasn't just the furnishings, which were lovely, but the location and the view and just the overall *feeling* of the place. It was indescribable. Especially for a city girl like her. She'd always preferred city views. A downtown high-rise hotel looking out on the skyline of a major city: that was what she'd preferred.

Maybe all that time, she'd been wrong. But maybe it wasn't just the mountains and the fresh air that was making her feel things she'd never felt before. Maybe it was only just a part of it?

There was a knock on the bathroom door. "Are you almost ready in there?"

Max waited for her in the living room of her suite while she went to change in preparation for their first adventure. She had a *living room.* "Almost," she called back. The truth was, she was nowhere near ready. But at this point, she didn't think she'd ever be ready for whatever Max had planned. Because the more time she spent with Max, the harder it was to lie to him. Maybe if she could just get him to sign off on their contract, declaring the job done, maybe then she could come clean to him?

Yeah, right, Tess. And maybe he won't totally hate you for lying to him all along.

Tess tugged her hair up into a ponytail. He was totally going to hate her. She either didn't say anything at all and squash the feelings she was undeniably starting to have. Or she could tell him the truth and he'd hate her. Either way, she lost.

"Nice job, Tess. You've really screwed things up this time." Her reflection in the mirror gave nothing away. With one last sigh, she pasted on her best *I'm ready for this* smile and headed out to meet Max and see what he had lined up for her.

When she finally emerged into the main room of her suite, Max had his back to the room and stood at the picture window, staring out at the mountain. Like a clichéd movie scene, she paused and watched him a moment, using the opportunity to check him out without his noticing.

If circumstances were different...

No. There was no point thinking about it. They would never work out, anyway. Whoever said opposites attract clearly didn't live in the real world. Even if there was a mutual attraction, and no extraneous circumstances, it would never work. There was no point giving it any more thought.

"Ready?"

He turned around and smiled. "Always. And you look substantially more ready for some time in the outdoors than you did the other day."

Tess laughed because she knew the words *ready for time in the outdoors* was a huge stretch. She'd scoured the depths of her closet for something that looked remotely as though it could pass for "mountain adventure" gear. She wasn't sure her pink plaid shirt and oldest jeans did the trick, but it was the best she could do. "Honestly, this type of thing isn't usually something I'm prepared for."

"You don't say." He winked at her as he walked past. When

his hand brushed hers, thrills shot up her arm. "But you look great, and absolutely perfect for what I have in mind today."

She followed him across the room and out the front door, stopping only long enough to grab a bottle of water. It wasn't until she was sitting next to him in an open top Jeep that she thought to ask him what exactly he had in mind for the day.

Having her sit so close to him, smelling so damn good, it took all Max had to focus on the rough road as they bumped along. Every once in a while, Tess bounced up in the seat and grabbed the handle to hold herself still. "Sorry the road is so rough," he said, not really sorry at all. Watching her trying to keep her composure was one of the cutest things he'd seen in a long time. And it didn't hurt that the tank top she wore under the ridiculous plaid shirt—that was thankfully unbuttoned just enough to notice—was nice and snug on her curves. "Normally I'd start hiking right from the Lodge but given that you don't have a lot of experience in the woods, I thought it might be better to drive some of the way. It was that or a horse ride, which I could—"

"No. The Jeep is fine."

He couldn't help it; he laughed at her. "Don't tell me you've never been on a horse either?" He shook his head. "Man, that bio of yours really is a piece of fiction."

Tess's lips pressed into a thin line. "It's not that it's fiction…"

"It's just that it's totally fabricated." He grinned and decided to push a little harder. "I have to think that it's not very ethical to misrepresent yourself that way. What else have you misrepresented yourself about? Are you really a business consultant? What exactly is your expertise in advising on this type of job?" Her eyes were wide, and he could see a flash of panic reflected there. It wasn't his intention to upset her; he just wanted the truth. No, he *needed* the truth. "I'm pretty sure we hired you based on the information in your bio," he continued. "After all, you present yourself not only as an expert of business analysis, but on an adventure lifestyle. On paper, you were the perfect person for this job. But in real life..."

"What are you saying, Max?" She turned in her seat and stared at him.

He had to admire her courageousness. She was clearly in a losing situation, but she wasn't giving in.

"What I'm saying is that I think you've been misrepresenting yourself."

She took a deep breath. "Okay."

"Okay?"

"I'll tell you the—oh my God. What's that?"

Max slammed on the brakes with her outburst and turned around to see what she was pointing at.

"Is that a..."

"A moose." He put his hand on hers in an effort to calm her because it was indeed a beautiful bull moose, standing just through the trees off the road and watching them. "I can't remember the last time I was so close to one." He kept his voice low. "Good eye. I would have missed him."

"Is he...will he..."

Max slipped his hand around hers and squeezed to keep it from trembling. "He won't hurt us. He's just curious. Kind of like we are. As long as we don't spook him and he doesn't feel threatened, it'll be fine."

The animal was magnificent, but his strong presence had nothing on the beauty sitting next to Max.

"You've never seen a moose before?"

She shook her head, her eyes fixed on the creature. But Max only had eyes for her and the wonderment on her face as she gazed at the animal. "I've seen an elk," she said. "And deer of course."

"Of course." Max tried not to smile.

"But...wow. It's...I just can't..."

He was so caught up watching Tess watch the moose that Max didn't even realize he'd started to stroke the top of her hand with his thumb. It was completely inappropriate, but it felt right in that moment.

And then the moment was over.

"Oh," she said. "He's leaving."

By the time Max turned around to see, he could only make out the retreating form of the huge animal moving away. As big as they were, moose could move very quickly, and shockingly quietly. Not that he would have noticed if the creature had made a huge noise—Max was way too fixated on Tess.

"That was so cool." Tess pulled her hand away from his, and immediately Max wanted to pull it back, and pull her back. Closer to him. Much closer. With an effort, he placed both his hands on the steering wheel to keep from reaching out to her again and continued the drive to the trailhead. For the rest of the drive, Tess chattered on about the moose and how she'd wished she had a camera.

"We're here," Max announced as he pulled the Jeep into a small clearing on the side of the road.

"We're where?" Tess propped herself up on her hands and peered around. "I don't see anything. I thought you were going to show me—"

"The potential site for the zip line," he finished. "Come on. We better get a move on if we're going to make it in and out before dinner."

Tess got out of the Jeep and looked around again. There was nothing but towering pine trees and…well, forest around her. They were definitely not anywhere near a site for a zip line. They were absolutely in the middle of nowhere. She walked around the vehicle to find Max pulling backpacks out of the backseat.

"Here." He handed her a pack, which she almost dropped. "This is yours."

"For what?"

"To carry. It has water and snacks and a first aid kit."

"First aid?"

Max swung his own pack over his back with ease and walked toward the trees.

"Why do I need first aid?"

"You don't," he said without turning around. "And hopefully you won't. But you never know. It's best to be prepared before going into the wilderness."

"Wilderness?" The word was stupid. It was even more stupid that she said it out loud when she was, in fact, surrounded by wilderness. But she was having trouble wrapping her head around what was going on. "You said we were going to see the site?"

"Yes." He turned around and stared at her with barely contained amusement. "We are. But we have to hike there. I normally hike up from the Lodge but I figured you might not be up to such a long trek. It's not far from here, though. Are you up to it?"

Tess didn't actually know whether she was or not, but she wasn't about to tell Max that. It was bad enough he thought she was a huge liar for fabricating her bio.

But you ARE a liar! And it had nothing to do with the bio.

Her head spun with all the lies that were piling up on one another. She was getting in way too deep for what was supposed to be a simple in and out assignment and she was seriously questioning whether it was worth it.

"Of course I'm up to it." She quickly swung the heavy pack onto her back and caught up with him.

His hand reached out and brushed her shoulder. "Here," he said. "Let me adjust that for you." Max slid his fingers under the straps over her shoulders, and pulled and tugged until the backpack felt significantly more comfortable, the weight of it almost gone. "Better?"

"Much."

He hesitated for a beat. His hand lingered on her arm; their eyes connected and she could see that whatever was going on between them was much more than just a work arrangement. She had to say something. "Max, I…"

Tess swallowed hard. Max blinked.

"You what?"

"I…" She forced a smile. "I'm excited for my first hike."

He laughed, but the sound didn't ring true. "Well then, let's get started."

Chapter Six

TESS ACTUALLY TURNED out to be a decent hiker, not that it really surprised him. After all, she was in great shape. A fact that he enjoyed as she hiked in front of him. Her jeans hugged her curves in all the right places as she scrambled up some of the steeper sections. He could have taken her on the lower trail, but it wouldn't have been nearly as much fun if he couldn't put his hands on her waist to help her up the rocky portions of the trail. No, he'd definitely made the right choice.

It didn't take long for them to get to the first clearing where he'd envisioned building the base camp and first tower for the zip line. "So?" he asked. "What do you think?"

He watched as Tess took in the site. He didn't really have to ask what she was thinking, because he could see it all over her face. Besides, he knew the site was perfect. The trees opened up into a small valley over a creek where the zip lines could stretch across to give guests the most spectacular views. With the mountains towering all around them, it was like a little piece of paradise tucked away and it would be absolutely perfect. He'd always thought so. From the moment he'd first laid eyes on the valley, he'd known a zip line and treetop park would be just the thing to add a little adventure for the guests of Castle Mountain Lodge; he just didn't actually think he could pull it off. Not until Clara's report. Or Tess, delivering Clara's report…whatever. And then after she'd tried it back in Breckenridge, and he'd seen her reaction, Max knew. He could give that to hundreds of others just like her. Guests who never thought they could do something so wild. So out of their wheelhouse.

Tess had taught him that.

"This is amazing, Max." She shook her head in wonderment. "You could put the first tower right there." She pointed to the exact spot Max had picked out. "And maybe on that side, you could build some rope course activities to challenge guests before another line back to this side."

"That's a great idea, Te—Clara." He corrected himself quickly and then for good measure, added, "I don't care what your bio says—you're really good at your job."

She laughed and in doing so, stumbled backward. Max caught her quickly and pulled her close to keep her from toppling down the slope. "I got you."

And did he ever. She fit perfectly in his arms and he certainly wasn't in a hurry to let her go. Especially when she turned so her face was only inches away from his. Her heart beat so rapidly he could feel it against his chest. He should have let her go. He should have stepped back and set her on her feet.

But he wasn't doing any of that.

Not. A. Chance.

She licked her lips as he bent his head to hers. That slight action broke the last bit of resolve he had. Max's lips crashed onto hers. He held her tight as he explored her mouth with his, tasting every inch of her. And she kissed him back. Oh, did she ever. If there was any doubt that she might have similar feelings for him, they were completely blown away with the way her mouth moved on his.

A small moan escaped her lips as Max slipped his hand up and under her shirt to the smooth skin of her back. Her skin was warm, and soft and oh, so smooth. It took every bit of restraint that he could muster to stop himself from letting his hands circle around her waist to her front.

No. He had to be patient. There was still so much to discover between them.

Like her name.

That annoying voice of reason piped up from deep inside him and he paused; his lips stilled on hers. Not long, but long enough to catch her attention.

"Max?" She pulled back, but he didn't release her. "What's—"

"Nothing." He kissed her again but it wasn't enough to close out the little voice in his mind that kept reminding him that there were still too many secrets between them.

Dammit.

Reluctantly he pulled away and put his hand to his mouth, either in an effort to hold onto the memory of the feel of her lips on his, or to let it go. Either way, what he really wanted to do was turn around and grab her again. She fit so perfectly in his arms, none of the rest of it mattered.

Except it did.

It really did.

Max wasn't the type of guy to start something he couldn't finish and there was no way he could start anything at all with a woman who couldn't be honest with him. Especially about the most basic of things.

Like who she was.

What the hell?

Tess stood for a minute, stunned at what had just happened.

And what *had* just happened?

One minute Max had his arms around her and was kissing her. And, oh, was he ever kissing her. And the next minute… nothing. He'd literally pushed her away.

He stared out over the valley, so Tess took the chance to run her hands through her hair in an effort to compose herself. Not that it helped—exactly the opposite. Her head spun with how quickly things had changed. There was no way she could have made up the chemistry between them. Especially when he was the one to kiss *her*.

What she should do was demand an explanation. It wasn't okay to be treated that way. It wasn't okay to…oh, who was she kidding? Righteous indignation wasn't her thing. Especially considering she owed him an explanation. A huge one. And it had never been more clear than it was in that moment.

She turned and walked a few feet away toward the tree line and the path that she assumed would lead her back to the Jeep. Not that she had any intention of heading out on her own. She wasn't that stupid. But she did need a little distance. Even if it was only a few feet. It was something. And given the swirl of feelings going through her at the moment, distance was the best thing for her. She had no right to be hurt, but at the same time, she had every right.

It was too—

"We should probably head back."

Tess managed a nod. "Yes. If you think you've shown me everything I need to see."

"You tell me, Clara."

Was it her imagination, or did he emphasize her name? *Did he know? Could he possibly know?*

Tess ran her hand through her hair in an effort to

straighten her ponytail and compose herself. Of course he could know the truth; she was a terrible actress and an even worse business consultant. The whole trip had been a bad idea. All she was doing was making things worse.

She nodded again but didn't say anything.

"Right."

When Max walked past her to take the lead on the trail, her body reacted immediately to his closeness. Every nerve ending was on alert and her body yearned to reach out to him. Not that she could. She was afraid she'd never be able to touch him again. And after that kiss they'd just shared, that was the only thing she wanted.

But whatever had happened between them on the ridge a moment ago had changed things and the worst part was…Tess had no idea what it was. Sure, she'd managed to screw things up to an extent that she wouldn't have imagined but he didn't know that. Not yet anyway. But one thing she did know for sure: once he did know the truth, everything was just going to get worse.

They hiked for a few minutes in silence, which gave Tess the unfortunate opportunity to get caught up in her own thoughts. That was never a good idea because that meant she was overthinking everything.

How could she feel about Max the way she did after such a short time? More than that, how could she allow herself to develop any feelings at all when she was pretending to be someone she wasn't? And wasn't he obviously feeling something too? After all, *he* was the one who kissed *her*.

He'd also been the one to push her away.

Why?

That one word replayed in her head over and over until it completely consumed her. She didn't see the root that stuck up on the path and tripped her, causing her to tumble, hands flailing, right into the back of Max, who, caught off guard, couldn't catch himself. Together they fell to the forest floor with a thud. Max took the brunt of the impact, landing flat on his back with Tess on top of him. His arm threaded around her back to hold her close. Their faces were only inches apart and Tess knew she shouldn't do it. After all, she had him at a disadvantage, but that's exactly why she *should* do it.

Before she could give it any more thought, Tess leaned down and closed the distance between them, pressing her lips to his. She kissed him hard, and judging by the groan that he made, followed by the tightening of his arms around her body, he wasn't objecting to her forwardness. She pulled back just enough to look into his eyes and the want reflected back at her. She didn't have a chance to say anything before Max threaded his fingers through her hair and pulled her back down to his mouth. And then, all at once, there were hands everywhere, and his lips on hers, and then they were on her neck and his hands moved under her t-shirt. Every inch of her skin was on fire with his touch.

With a grunt and a move that left her breathless, Max flipped her over so he was on top of her, his arms on either side of her. His eyes were full of heat as they stared down at her. Instead of letting herself think of all the reasons they shouldn't be doing what they were doing, all Tess could think of was all the reasons they should. Primarily because of the insane attraction between them.

Was there anything wrong with that?

She licked her lips and he bent to kiss them.

No. There was nothing wrong with it.

Except, then he was hesitating again. His lips stilled on hers and he pulled back. "We shouldn't do this."

She shook her head. "It's okay, Max. I'm not…"

"You're not what?" He watched her, the question in his eyes.

If his objection was that they were working together and it

was a conflict of interest, she could end that right now. All she had to do was tell the truth.

It was so simple. She bit her lip just hard enough to feel the sting of it. "I…I'm not sure what I was going to say." She lied and gave him the sweetest smile she could manage before she swallowed hard and added, "But if you don't think we should be doing this, I just want to tell you that I really don't see a reason why we shouldn't. After all, we're both consenting adults. There's really no—"

"What I meant was that we shouldn't be doing this *here*." Max pushed himself up and held a hand out to her, which she took. As soon as she was on her feet, he pulled her into a hug. "I want to take you out, Clara. I want to show you everything the Lodge has to offer. Not just the beauty of the forest."

She kissed his cheek chastely. "That sounds amazing."

And it did, too. All except the part where he'd called her Clara.

Chapter Seven

"YOU CAN'T TELL HIM."

Tess paced the living room of her suite for at least the tenth time with her cell phone pressed to her ear. She'd known it would do no good to ask Clara about telling Max the truth. In fact, she should have trusted her instinct and just gone with her gut. With Clara, it was often easier to beg for forgiveness rather than ask for permission. But the guilt had gotten the best of her and she'd picked up her phone.

"I have to tell him, Clara. I don't think you understand."

"Oh no." Clara's voice came through loud and clear despite the fact she was calling from thousands of miles away. It was just her luck that they had a clear connection. It would have been so much easier if Tess could claim a misunderstanding due to static on the line. "Castle Mountain Lodge is a huge account. I mean, huge, Tess. You can't screw it up."

Tess stopped short. "Wait. If it was such a *huge* account, why am I here?" Hadn't Clara told her it was no big deal? A no-brainer? In fact, weren't those her exact words? "Shouldn't you be here taking care of *your* business if it's such a big deal?"

"I knew you could handle it."

"More like, you wanted to go to Europe with your latest sugar daddy more than you wanted to handle your very important account?" Tess knew it was a low blow, but she didn't care. As every day went on, she got more and more upset as it became crystal-clear that Clara had set her up for disaster. "I know you were trying to do me a favor, Clara." She took a deep breath and tried to keep things in perspective. "And I really appreciate it. I do. But I think things have gone a bit too far."

There was a beat of silence on the other end and for a moment, Tess was sure they'd been disconnected. But then Clara said, "What do you mean, things have gone too far?"

Oh crap. Tess spun in a circle, looking for something to help her out of telling the truth to her best friend, but the empty hotel suite offered up no assistance.

"Tess?"

"Um...well...it's not..."

"Tess, *what* has gone too far? What's happened? Please tell me my account is okay. Castle Mountain Lodge is—"

"I know, I know. It's a big account." Tess rolled her eyes. "Which I still don't understand. But it's fine. I think..."

"What do you mean, you think? Tess! It was easy. I set it all up for you. All you had to do was go through the file."

"No, Clara." Tess stamped her foot on the floor. "That is *not* all I had to do. He wanted me to come back here and see the site, Clara. The *site*. What do I know about a site? Nothing. I know nothing about the site. I know nothing about adventure travel. I know nothing about any of this. I'm just trying to do my best and not screw things up too badly for you because I know this is your business and it's important to you and it's important to me, too, because you know I need the money. But you know what else is important to me? Not lying. Not telling someone I'm somebody I'm not. I'm not good at it, Clara. In fact, I'm really, really bad at it. And what's more is that I don't want to be good at it. All I want to do is tell him the truth about who I am because you know what, I'm a nice person and he's a nice person. Except I'm *not* a nice person because I've been lying to him about who I am when all I really want is for him to know who I *really* am because I like him. I like him a lot. I might even be falling in love with him."

She tossed the phone onto the counter as if it were hot and would burn her. Her hand flew to her mouth. *Did she really just say all that? Out loud?*

"Tess?"

She shook her head at the phone even though there was no one there to see it.

"Tess?!"

She swallowed and picked up the phone again. "I'm here." She was trying for a level of calm that she certainly didn't feel. She'd just admitted to her best friend that she might actually be falling in love with their client. The same client who thought she was Clara.

"You're falling in love with Maxwell Grant?"

Tess nodded but didn't say anything. But she didn't have to.

"Really?"

"Yes," she said after a minute. "I really think I am."

"Well then, that changes things," Clara said matter-of-factly.

"It does?"

"Of course."

Tess's head spun. "Do you mean I should tell him? What about your account? Don't you think he'll be upset and fire you from the account?"

"Honestly? I don't know. What do *you* think will happen?"

"I...I'm not..." Tess swallowed hard. "I'm actually not sure."

"Where do things stand right now?"

"I encouraged him to put in a zip line and he showed me the site."

"What? He wants to put in a zip line? That wasn't in the proposal I gave you."

That was a small detail she'd forgotten all about. "I know it wasn't, Clara. But have you ever actually been on a zip line? It's amazing and I can't imagine how it wouldn't be a good thing to put in. I mean, it's so—"

"Wait. You went on a zip line? *YOU?*"

"Well…it's not like I had a choice. He thought I was you. He said I needed to experience it before I could make a decision so we went to Glacier Ridge Adventures and did it. It's crazy cool, though."

"And you liked it?"

"I loved it."

She was starting to get annoyed by the incredulous tone in her friend's voice. Sure, she wasn't known for her wild antics but it wasn't as if Tess didn't ever do anything fun. It wasn't *totally* out of the realm of possibilities.

Tess could almost hear Clara shaking her head on the other end of the phone. "Well, I'm glad you liked it," she said after a minute. "But you have to tell him it's a bad idea."

"What's a bad idea?"

"A zip line. Haven't you been listening?"

Yes, she was listening. Tess's head was spinning from all the things that weren't good ideas.

"A zip line is a terrible idea, Tess. If you read through the file, you'll see that the logistics of installing such a thing is too much and then there's the cost. Never mind the fact that the Lodge has always positioned itself as being a romantic destination. *Not* an adventure center."

"I know," Tess said. "I read it five times. But isn't that why they hired us? To help *create* an adventure center?"

"Us?"

Tess flinched, but didn't back down. "Yes, *us*. After all, I'm sort of you right now."

"Maybe so, but if you really were me, you wouldn't be recommending something that could potentially be destroying my company. Really, Tess. If they take this ridiculous recommendation and go with it just to have it fail, I'll be ruined."

She hadn't thought of that. Of course, she hadn't thought of *any* of that. She hadn't thought of it because it wasn't her business. She wasn't a consultant; she wasn't trained in anything to do with advising people on what they should do with their companies, and she certainly didn't know what she was doing when it came to adventure and zip lines. If Clara wanted to be angry at her, she could be, but if anyone should be angry about anything, it should be her.

"But I'm *not* you, Clara. That's the whole point." Tess stopped her pacing and opened the patio door. The fresh mountain air washed over her but it didn't do anything to help her calm down. "I've been trying my best because you asked me to, and because you know I need the money. But I'm not you, Clara. I'm not. And I'm going to make mistakes and screw up and I'm sorry, but if you wanted things done a certain way, you should have done them yourself. It's not fair for you to get upset with me when all I'm doing is trying my best." She dropped her head in her hands. "And I'll tell you another thing. I love you, but I'm so mad at you right now. I can't do this anymore. I just can't."

She hung up before Clara could respond. She didn't want to hear what her friend had to say. Her cell phone rang a second later, just the way she knew it would. Clara's face filled the screen. Tess reached down and switched it off right before she realized they'd never finished discussing telling Max the truth.

"A zip line?"

Ryan Morrison, the customer service manager, and the first ally Max had when he moved to the Lodge, stared at him over a beer with a look that would have been laughable if Max wasn't so serious. When Ryan invited Max to join him and Bo, the outdoor activities director, for a few beers after their shift, he'd jumped at the opportunity. Mostly because he needed some space from Tess to think about his next step, and also because he was going to be working closely with these men and building a relationship with them was definitely not a bad idea.

"Yes, a zip line. Why not?"

Ryan laughed and Bo shook his head, but remained silent. "Offhand?" Ryan held up a hand and ticked off fingers. "I can think of about fifteen different reasons." He waved his hands in the air, having run out of fingers. "Not the least of which will be the fact that no one will want to use it."

"I don't think that's true." Max picked up his beer and took a long pull. "I think lots of people will want to try it out."

"No way." Ryan shook his head. "If anyone knows the guests and what they want, it's me. They want romance. They want relaxation. They want—"

"Adventure," Max finished for him.

Bo laughed, but still didn't say anything. He focused intently on his beer.

"That's why I was brought on, Ryan. Management wants adventure brought to the Lodge. And that's what I'm going to do."

"I know, but I don't think it's a good idea. Especially not a zip line. You're going to bring in something like that…it's going to cost a crap load of money to put it in and at the end of the day, nobody is going to want to do it because it requires too much energy."

"Energy?"

"Absolutely. The Lodge is about relaxing and the entire experience that goes along with that. If it requires too much energy, they won't want to do it."

"I don't think that's true." Max could feel himself getting heated. He liked Ryan; he really did. But what he didn't like was the fact that the man couldn't see the bigger picture. All he could see was what was in front of him. And there was so much opportunity being left on the table. "Bo? What do you think?"

The other man set down his beer and rubbed a hand over his chin. He took a minute to think things over, but Max knew he already had an opinion. How could he not?

"I don't disagree," Bo said finally.

"What do you mean?" Ryan looked between them. "You don't disagree with who?"

"With either of you." He picked his beer up again and drained it before he set it down again. "I think you both have valid points."

Max took a deep breath. His relaxing beers with the guys was quickly turning into an exercise in frustration. "But if you had a vote in it," he pushed, "what would it be?"

"Well, that's the thing, guys." Bo laughed and pushed up from the table. "I *don't* have a say in it. Besides, isn't that what you hired a consultant for? Where is she anyway? Rumor has it you brought her to the Lodge."

"He did." Ryan leaned back in his chair, a grin across his face. He obviously liked the change of topic. "And she's cute. Clara Clark. Not at all what I expected in a business consultant, but hey, I'd—"

"Don't finish that sentence," Max warned. The intense flare of protectiveness that flashed through him took him by surprise. If anyone was going to think about his consultant in a way that was anything but professional, it was going to be him.

His consultant.

"Just…don't finish it."

The smile faded from the other man's face, replaced by a knowing smirk. "And why would that be, Max?"

Bo placed his hands on each of their shoulders and stood between them. "I think we all know why that is. Can I give you a bit of advice, Max?"

He looked up and shook Bo's hand off him. "Go for it."

"I should tell you not to get involved with someone you work with, but at the end of the day, it actually worked out well for me. So what I am going to tell you is to be careful."

Careful. That was Bo's big advice? Max didn't know what he expected, but he definitely expected more than that from the man. It was well known that Bo and his fiancée Morgan were one of the greatest love stories of Castle Mountain Lodge. They'd fallen in love over Bo's young daughter, Ella, when Morgan came to work in the Cub Club, the children's center, and they'd made it work.

It's not that he was looking for advice, but if he was going to get some, he figured Bo would be a good source.

"I think it's a terrible idea." Ryan leaned back in his chair.

"Didn't you meet your girlfriend at the Lodge?" Bo lifted his glass and smiled over the edge.

"That's different," Ryan said. "We don't work together."

"Not technically."

Max looked between the two men but didn't say anything.

"Besides, she's clearly not your type," Ryan said after a moment.

Possessiveness rose up in him and it took all he had not to reach across the table and punch the man's smile off.

"I don't have time for this." Bo shook his head with a laugh. "You boys can sort it out."

As far as Max was concerned, there was nothing to sort out. Not where Tess was concerned. *Except for the very minor detail*

of the lie between them. But after that kiss in the woods this afternoon, he was more than done with the games they were playing. And that's exactly why he had a special dinner planned for
them in the village later. It was time to see whether there was
anything real between them.

No. It was way past time.

Chapter Eight

TESS HAD TAKEN a bit of extra care getting ready for dinner. It wasn't entirely because of Max either. Not really. She'd always been of the opinion that when you had something particularly challenging to deal with, it was always a good idea to present yourself in the best possible way. If you looked confident, you might actually feel confident. It didn't always work, but she needed all the help she could get, so she was willing to try anything.

And she did feel good as she walked into the main Lodge building.

Max had invited her out for dinner. His message had said he needed to talk to her about something. Well, if Max thought he needed to talk, was he ever in for a surprise. If anyone needed to get something off her chest, it was her. After her conversation with Clara, Tess had never been so certain.

She was done lying. If Clara was worried about her business, she should get her ass to Castle Mountain Lodge herself and advise, the way she was supposed to be doing. But as far as Tess was concerned, she couldn't go one more minute pretending to be someone she wasn't. It wasn't fair to Max. For so many reasons. Sure, she could flub her way through the advising role, and maybe it would be different if that's all there was to it. But that wasn't all. Not even close.

She was falling in love with him. It was ridiculous to even think that when she'd only known him for a few days and he was the exact opposite of everything she'd ever wanted, and he was definitely the opposite of everything she *was*. But she couldn't help it. There was something between them. Some kind of connection, an electricity. She couldn't even describe it. But she didn't have to because when they kissed, it was all there. She'd never felt like that after a kiss and what was more…Tess knew he felt it, too. You couldn't fake that kind of chemistry. There was no way.

But even if Max was feeling something for her, right now he thought it was Clara he had those feelings for. Or had a connection with…or whatever. That wasn't the point. The point was she was *not* Clara and it was time that Max knew the truth. And the truth was exactly what he was going to get. Just as soon as she—

"Clara!"

Tess jolted with the shock of her name that wasn't her name and the touch on her shoulder.

"Oh, I'm sorry I startled you." A woman, immaculately dressed in a pant suit and bright pink blouse, stood in front of her with a smile that both impressed and scared Tess a little bit. "I called your name twice," the woman said. "But you didn't seem to hear me. I really didn't mean to scare you."

"Oh no." Tess waved her hand and tried her best to look in control. "You didn't startle me," she lied. "I was lost in thought is all. It's just so beautiful here and so easy to get distracted, don't you think?"

"I do." The woman tilted her head and every strand of her black hair moved in perfect unison. If there had ever been a more polished woman in her presence before, Tess couldn't think of who it might have been. "That's why I took the job and moved up here."

"Took the job? I'm sorry, do I know you?"

"Melissa Kramer." The woman stuck her hand out, which Tess took in a firm handshake, but not before she noticed Melissa's perfectly manicured nails that somehow matched the shade of her blouse perfectly. "I'm the general manager here at Castle Mountain Lodge. We spoke on the phone when I hired you."

Oh. My. God. Not again.

Tess worked hard to keep the panic off her face. "Of course." For half a second, Tess entertained the idea of telling this woman the truth. It would be good practice, and ultimately she was going to know everything soon enough. She forced a smile she most certainly didn't feel. "It's so nice to meet you, Melissa."

Melissa nodded. "I trust you've been enjoying the Lodge and Max has been taking good care of you?"

Oh, he's been taking care of me.

Tess smiled as sweetly as she could. "Absolutely. It's incredible here. Really, it's exceeded my expectations."

"Surely, you knew what to expect after talking to me on the phone." Melissa tilted her head in that way that people who knew something but didn't want to say they knew what they knew did.

But Tess was committed to the lie, at least for the time being, so she dug deep and channeled confidence she most certainly didn't feel.

"To an extent." Tess crossed her arms, mostly to keep them from shaking, but also in an effort to appear even slightly more put together than she felt. "But I have to tell you, Ms. Kramer—"

"Melissa."

"Melissa." She continued smoothly. "You really didn't do

the Lodge justice. I mean, yes…you explained it very well on the phone." Tess took a stab in the dark that she actually had done so. "But there is something about this place that you just cannot convey verbally, don't you agree?"

The other woman opened her mouth, likely to object, but then closed it again, pressed her lips together and finally nodded. "I agree."

"And now that I'm actually here, breathing in the fresh pine air, experiencing the brilliant blue skies and the mountains that simply go on forever…well, I must tell you. It really does give me an entirely different respect for what Castle Mountain Lodge is, what it really has to offer and of course, the potential for even more offerings with an adventure travel component."

Melissa regarded her for a moment and Tess did her best to swallow any and all panic that she was going to be caught out. Finally, after what seemed like hours, Melissa smiled, the first warm, genuine smile Tess had seen from her. "I'm so glad you really understand the Lodge and what we're trying to do here. I have to admit, when I was hired on as the general manager and asked to bring in something different, I was afraid that we might risk losing the feel of the place. When I found Max and brought him on, I just felt he was the right fit, but I have to be honest…"

Tess had a feeling that she probably wasn't going to like what Melissa had to say.

"I wasn't sure about you, Clara."

Tess kept the smile pasted to her face and waited.

"I'll admit, it was my idea to hire you. Max didn't want anything to do with it. But it's important to do your due diligence in this type of situation, don't you agree?"

"Absolutely."

"Honesty and integrity in any business partner is extremely important," Melissa continued, as if she hadn't spoken. "And you do appear to have that."

If she only knew. "If I may ask," Tess said before she could think better or it, "what was it that you weren't sure about?"

Melissa paused a moment and tapped one of those pink nails against her lip. "I can't really put my finger on it, Clara. I'll tell you, I'm a very upfront, no nonsense type of woman."

"I get that impression."

"And I'm usually a very good judge of character. But there was something that didn't sit well with me. Ultimately, though, I trusted my gut and decided to proceed, and I must tell you, I'm glad I did. You seem like a very competent advisor, Ms. Clark, and like I said, you seem to have a solid understanding of the culture here at Castle Mountain Lodge. I look forward to your report. And what the two of you come up with."

Tess couldn't help feeling as if she was being dismissed, which she likely was. And it was with a mixture of annoyance and relief that she shook the other woman's hand once more, promised the report within a few days and made her escape down the hall to the front lobby where she was to meet Max, more confused than ever. If she came clean now, it really could risk everything.

"I hope this is okay." Max held out the chair for Tess. She looked amazing. He didn't think she could look any better than she had that afternoon in her jeans but dressed in a form-fitting blue dress that matched her eyes perfectly, she was simply knockout gorgeous. "Oliver's is the best in the village and the chef is amazing. I mean, the Lodge restaurants are excellent, too. But I wanted to show you the village up here as well. Maybe after we eat, we can walk and get a cappuccino from the little coffee shop?"

"Really," she sat, "this is perfect. It's all too much, really. I didn't expect you to take me out. After all, this is a business trip and—"

"Actually," he interrupted her. "I don't think we should talk about business tonight. In fact, I'd like to think of tonight as maybe a..."

Dare he call it a date? He'd never been the type to skirt around the issue or play games; there was no point starting now.

"A date," he finished as he sat across from her. "If that's okay with you?"

She was silent for so long, he worried maybe he'd read her wrong. Read *everything* wrong. But no, there was no way he'd read that kiss wrong.

Finally, she nodded and smiled. "Okay. A date. But there's something I should tell you first."

"Don't tell me you're married?" He laughed, and instantly regretted it when he saw the look on her face.

"No," she said slowly. "It's not that. But I really do..."

That was it. She was going to tell him the truth and they could finally move forward with whatever it was that was going on between them. He held his breath and waited.

And waited.

After a moment, her face shifted; the frown morphed into a sweet smile. "You know what? It's nothing." She grabbed her napkin off the table and fluffed it onto her lap just as the waitress appeared to take their drink order.

Max ordered a bottle of red wine with barely a glance at the wine menu and turned his attention back to Tess. She hadn't told him. It was her chance to come clean and he'd been so sure that she would. After all, they couldn't move forward with whatever was going on between them if she didn't. It looked more and more like he'd have to force the issue.

"I'm really looking forward to a nice, relaxing evening, Max. There's been so much emphasis on work lately. I absolutely agree with you: let's not talk about work or anything to do with it."

Including the fact that you're not really the consultant we hired. There was no point saying it out loud, he realized. Not if he wanted to enjoy his evening with her. And he did. More than anything, he did.

"I couldn't agree more. So, tell me...when you aren't consulting for the business of which we will not speak, what *are* you doing? What's your favorite way to spend your free time?"

He leaned back in his chair and watched her beautiful face light up as she started to talk.

"You're going to think it's stupid."

"I assure you, I won't."

She laughed self-consciously and bit her lip. "Well, I know you're Mr. Adventure, and in your spare time you probably summit mountains and swing from vines in the forest."

He shrugged. Only one of those things was true, but he didn't need to point that out. Not yet anyway.

"You're going to think that that my hobbies are boring and mundane."

"I assure you, I'm not." And he knew he wouldn't. The more time he spent with her, the more Max realized that although on the surface she wasn't a daredevil or adventurer like he was, she was so much more, in so many ways. And she didn't even know it. So much so that she felt she had to pretend to be someone she wasn't. But as much as he still didn't know about the real Tess, she was definitely not boring or mundane, and she was definitely worth getting to know better. "I want to know," he insisted. "I want to know everything about you. And I can't imagine anything being less than thrilling when it comes to you."

She blushed all the way down her neck into the dip of cleavage on her dress. Max made no effort to hide his gaze as he followed the trail of flushed skin.

She reached for and took a sip of water. "Okay, but you have to promise not to laugh."

He crossed his heart with a finger. "Promise."

"Okay, well as you know, I live in Denver." Max nodded. "But I grew up spending my summers in Northern California with my grandma and even though I don't get the chance as often as I'd like, whenever I can, I make the drive so I can sit on the beach."

"Just sit?"

She nodded. "I know it's not very exciting, and I don't get there very often any more, but I kind of have a tradition when I go. I get a double latte and a day-old cinnamon bun from Barb's Barista Bar."

"Day old?"

She nodded and kept talking. "Then I walk. I do the same walk every time, but it's not boring and it's never the same because that's the crazy thing about the beach. It looks different every time. It's always changing. I like to collect sea glass. Even all these years later. I have a whole jar of it in my kitchen. It's kind of my hobby, trying to fill the jar. I'll do it everyday that I'm there, walk for hours if I can, and then when my trip is over, I'll come home with handfuls to add to my collection. But before I leave, I sit in the sand and throw pieces of cinnamon bun to the seagulls."

"Oh, you're one of those people."

She laughed, a sound like sunshine that lit him up from the inside. "What do you mean, one of *those* people?"

"You're one of those people who feed the birds and get them all in a frenzy, flying over my head ready to attack or…worse."

Tess laughed again. "I see. You're one of *those* people." She took a sip of her water and sat back as the waitress arrived with their wine. "You're afraid of birds." She whispered the words, but the waitress heard and did a terrible job of hiding a chuckle as she presented the wine.

Max obliged by tasting the wine and waiting for the waitress to pour them each a glass. When she was gone, he leaned across the table. "I wouldn't have to be one of those people if you weren't one of those people."

She laughed—it was a sound Max was quickly getting used to hearing—and raised her glass in a toast. "To..."

"Those people," he finished for her.

The night was going well. In fact, it was easily the best date Tess had had in years. Not that it was a date. Not really. But maybe it was. The way he looked at her, flirted with her, caught her hand in his when she was reaching for the salt... Yes, she decided. It was definitely a date. More than that, whatever weirdness had happened between them on the trail was gone.

In fact, Tess was positive that given the chance again, no one would be backing away from another kiss. Her body flushed with anticipation of his lips on hers again. His hands in her hair, his—

"Clara? Are you okay?"

She shook her head just enough to clear it and focus on Max. "Of course," she said. "I'm fine. I was just thinking." *Thinking about how good it would be to hear you say* my *name.*

That was it. It had gone on long enough. She'd just have to deal with whatever happened. Clara would understand.

Would she?

The image of the perfectly put together Melissa flashed through her mind. That was a woman who definitely would not understand if she found out she'd been deceived. No way.

But maybe it was a risk she'd have to take.

"I'm sorry," she said when she realized Max was waiting for an answer to a question she most certainly hadn't heard.

He smiled, as if he knew what she was thinking. *Maybe he did.* The thought crossed her mind like a bolt but instantly fizzled out. There was no way he knew she wasn't Clara. Max was definitely not the type of man to go along with something like that. He would have said something.

He reached across the table for her hand, a move that grounded her and brought her back into the moment. "I was just wondering if you'd like to walk up the main street with me and get a coffee? It's not much, really. In fact, it's kind of kitschy. Just a few gift shops, a flower shop that services the weddings at the Lodge, and a little café. They make the best cappuccinos, though. And you seem like you could use a coffee."

"I think that sounds great. Besides, it's a beautiful night for a walk and a little mountain air would do me some good. I'm feeling a little warm all of a sudden."

It wasn't a lie. Her entire body was flushed, no longer only due to his closeness but also from the risk she was about to take.

The fresh air *did* feel good and as they walked, Tess felt better and better. Whatever panic had overcome her back in the restaurant had dissipated. With a coffee in hand, they walked the length of the short street to the sitting area where benches and rocks had been placed with wildflowers growing all around. It was the perfect place to sit and watch the world go by, or to have a conversation that could potentially change everything.

No. It *would* change everything.

"Is something on your mind?" Max asked her as they sat.

She took a deep breath. There was no point putting it off any longer. "As a matter of fact, there is."

"You're going to tell me you wish you had some day-old bread to feed the birds, aren't you?" He slapped his hand on his thigh. "I knew I should have bought that muffin. It was looking a little stale. It would have been perfect." She couldn't help it; she laughed. "But we don't have seagulls up here in the mountains. You would have had to settle for the sparrows and chickadees. Or maybe if you were lucky, a crow would come by."

He mimicked the actions of tossing crumbs to the birds, and she couldn't contain her laughter any longer. He looked so ridiculous and only seemed to feed off her laughter, which grew stronger until she was clutching her stomach. "Stop." She choked back another laugh. "You're killing me."

Max grabbed her hand and squeezed. "I'd never want to do that." His tone turned serious and his free hand slipped up to her cheek. "You're beautiful. Especially when you're laughing. You looked so worried and stressed earlier—I just want to make you laugh."

She tensed slightly at his words.

"No." He stroked her cheek with his thumb. "Don't lose the smile, okay?"

"I need to tell you something." She blurted the words out before she could stop herself. "I'm not Clara Clark. I'm not a business consultant and I've been lying to you."

She managed to get the words out before the shame overtook her and she looked at her feet. But it wasn't all shame that she felt: it was also an intense sense of relief. The lie had been eating her up, more than she realized. And now, no matter what happened, at least she'd been honest. If Max wasn't interested in her after that, there was nothing she could do about it. But she could not start a relationship based on a lie. No matter what.

The prospect of *no matter what* got a little more real when Max didn't immediately respond to her confession. The silence between them grew until it seemed like hours had gone by. When he finally took her hand, squeezed it and reached over to tilt her chin up so her eyes met his, she thought she'd explode from the relief of it.

Looking in his eyes felt good. It felt right, but not nearly as right as it felt when he bent down to kiss her. The moment his lips met hers, every bit of tension she had been holding onto for the last week exploded in passion as their mouths moved against each other. His hands laced in her hair, holding her close as she melted into him. When they finally pulled apart and Tess could look into his eyes, she knew it would be okay. He didn't seem to care at all that she had lied to him. In fact, it didn't seem to have been a surprise when she'd told him the news. It was as if he'd already…

"Max?"

He nodded and tilted his head in question.

"Don't get me wrong. I mean, I'm not looking for any trouble where there doesn't seem to be any, but aren't you upset with me? I mean…aren't you even a little upset that I lied to you about who I was?"

He opened his mouth to say something but closed it again, pressing his lips into a line. He nodded once before he said, "I knew."

"You…wait…what?"

"I knew you weren't Clara. I knew you were pretending."

Her head spun while she tried to process what he'd just said. "What do you mean, you *knew*?"

"Just that." He sat back to put a bit of distance between them, but he held onto her hand and squeezed it tight. "I had a feeling something wasn't on the up-and-up right away. I mean, it was pretty clear early on that you weren't the same woman I'd been chatting with via email. I mean, you weren't nearly as confident about what you were talking about as you should have been. Considering you're a consulting expert and all." He smiled, but Tess didn't feel like joining in.

"When?"

"When what?"

"When did you know for sure?" The urge to pull her hand away from his grip was strong, but she needed to hear him out, too.

He scooted closer to her on the bench, clearly becoming aware that she was not pleased with him. "Honestly, right away. Especially when we went out to Glacier Ridge. I didn't think you were actually going to go through with the zip line, though. That was pretty impressive."

"Like I passed a test?"

If he noticed the tension in her voice, he didn't recognize the danger there.

"I guess it was sort of a test. Honestly, I thought you'd break down right away and tell me the truth but then when you agreed to come up here to Castle Mountain Lodge, I was even more impressed by your level of commitment. Truly, you may not have been all that good at your role, but you were committed. That's for damn sure."

"Committed?"

"Absolutely." He sat back, as if he was proud of her for her dedication in her deception.

The whole thing was more and more confusing to follow, but one thing wasn't confusing to Tess: the piece of information that he'd known that she wasn't who she said she was, and he'd pushed her to her limits anyway. For some reason, that upset her more than was probably reasonable. But she didn't care whether she was being unreasonable or not. It wasn't fair for him to have put her through any of that. He'd played games with her.

"I thought for sure when we boarded the plane that you'd crack."

"Crack?"

"I kept waiting for you to come out with the truth,"he continued, completely oblivious of her growing discomfort with him. "And then when we kissed, I—"

"That was all part of the plan?" She'd had enough. She jumped up from the bench and pulled away from his hand. It was too much. Knowing he was playing a game with her was one thing, but to know the kisses they'd shared were all part of the plan to get her to *crack*...that was too much. That hurt.

"Tess. Please, I—"

"So you do know my name?" She whirled around and faced him. "And when did you learn that little nugget? Did you place some kind of bet as to when I would tell you my name, too?"

"Bet? No." He stood and tried to grab her hand again, but she wasn't having any part of it. "Of course not, Tess. There were no bets. I wasn't playing any games with anyone. It was just... Tess."

She couldn't stand there for one more minute. The whole situation was ridiculous. He was the one who should have been upset with *her*. Logically, she knew that, but everything he was saying was so ridiculous that she couldn't process it fast enough. She looked at him one more time. Her heart cracked with the knowledge that she'd never been more than a game to him. She turned and ran away.

Chapter Nine

WHAT THE HELL had just happened? They'd had an amazing date, the best Max had ever had with easy conversation and laughter and just enough flirtation to drive him crazy, and then it was just about to be perfect because Tess was going to come clean with the truth and they were going to have a good laugh about what a ridiculous situation it all was and then he'd kiss her again, and...

But that's not how it went at all. She'd gotten mad.

Tess had gotten mad. Shouldn't it have been him?

When she'd run off, every bone in his body had yearned to go after her but his head was smarter than his heart and he let her go. She was upset and she needed a chance to cool off before he could talk any sense to her. Instead, he'd turned and taken one of the longer trails through the trees. The sun lingered in the sky; even in the mountains, it stayed light enough into the night that the trail should be safe. Besides, if anyone knew his way around the woods, it was Max. And the fact that he was likely to be alone on the trails was definitely appealing. He needed to clear his head.

The more he walked, the clearer it became. He'd gone too

far, and he knew the moment it had happened. It was all in her eyes. Her beautiful blue eyes. She'd been so concerned about telling him the truth. So worried. But then he'd been a jerk.

"Dammit." He kicked a rock and watched as it bounced into the woods and disappeared. That's why she'd run off. He'd been a total jerk. He should have pulled her close and told her it was okay and she must have her reasons for the lie. He should have listened. And he never should have played with her. He couldn't have seen it coming, but he was definitely the bad guy. And that was the very last thing he wanted.

He needed to find her. Because, yes, they were both in the wrong, but it was nothing that couldn't be fixed. And the only way to fix it was to be truthful. No more lies.

Max broke into a jog. He needed to stop her and find her before she went to bed. Or worse…left the Lodge.

"I'm leaving." Tess hadn't even waited until she got back to her suite before she called Clara. Her heels clicked on the stone pathway as she walked as quickly as she could without turning an ankle. "I'm sorry, but I have to leave. All of this was a bad idea and I'm just putting your business at risk." *And my heart*, she wanted to add.

"You can't leave. Not now."

"You don't understand." Tess sniffed back tears.

"No," Clara said. "I don't understand. I really don't, Tess. But I heard you when you said you were falling for this guy and I know you well enough to know that's something." Tess nodded even though her friend couldn't see. "And I'm still your best friend and as your best friend, I want to know everything about it, but…"

Of course there was a but.

"I need your help here." Tess took a breath and Clara continued. "Can we get through this? Can we——"

"Clara!"

Shit.

"Who's that?"

Tess turned to see Melissa striding toward her. She still looked impossibly put together, as if she'd just time warped through the last few hours without having lived at all. "It's Melissa Kramer," she hissed into the phone. "What the hell could she want? I talked to her earlier today." Tess wiped at her eyes with one hand and did her best to smooth her hair as the other woman came closer.

"You did? Keep me on the phone," Clara said. "I want to hear what's going on."

"Clara!" Melissa called again as she got closer. She moved at an incredible speed, but from what Tess could see as she got closer, there was zero sign of exertion. Not even a hair out of place or a bead of sweat. It was unreal.

"Tess." Clara spoke into her ear. "Keep the phone on, okay?"

"Okay." She agreed and held the phone down by her side, careful not to cover the microphone, as Melissa joined her.

"I'm glad I caught you," she said. "Were you headed somewhere?"

"Just on my way to bed," Tess said with a smile she most certainly didn't feel. "It's been a big day."

"Well, I won't keep you then. I just thought that since you're here, we might as well have the final recommendation meeting in person instead of over the phone like we originally discussed. I have an opening tomorrow morning. How does that work for you?"

"Tomorrow? Morning?"

"Yes. Is that a problem?"

Yes! That's a problem.

Tess smiled and nodded the way she'd been doing so much lately. "Not a problem at all," she said as sweetly as possible.

"I'm glad to hear it." Melissa tilted her head and examined Tess in a way that made her want to escape her skin. "Because as I'm sure you remember, honesty and integrity are very important to me when it comes to business and I would hate for you to tell me something if it wasn't true."

There was no doubt in Tess's mind that they were no longer talking about the meeting time. "Of course not, Melissa. In fact, tomorrow morning is perfect." Tess poured on every ounce of charm that she could muster. "I look forward to giving you my final report. I think you'll be pleased."

Melissa made a small noise that sounded strangely like a cross between a choke and a laugh. "Well, I'm not sure about pleased. But I'm fairly certain I'll be surprised. Rumor has it, you have some interesting ideas. I look forward to hearing them. Nine a.m.?"

"Perfect." Tess smiled through her teeth and waited until Melissa walked away before she brought the phone back up to her ear.

"Tess? Is she gone? What the hell?"

"She's gone." Tess sank down on a nearby bench. "I suppose you heard everything."

"I did."

A swirl of panic rose up inside her. Tess struggled to keep it at bay.

"What's she talking about?" Clara asked. "What kind of interesting ideas do you have? I thought we talked about this."

"We didn't talk about anything." Tess dropped her head into her hands. "You told me to read the file and I did that but then I went on the zip line and I—"

"Please tell me you didn't recommend a zip line."

"Well, not yet."

"Tess. We talked about this. I told you not to do it! All of the research I did and the data analysis…" Clara continued as if she hadn't spoken. "It's not feasible. It would be way too much money and the base would be too far from the Lodge to make a go of it. It doesn't make sense. You can't suggest it. I told you that."

"I don't think it's that bad of—"

"Tess. You can't. If they tried that and it failed it would be a disaster."

Something in her friend's words triggered her. What if *she* tried something and it failed? What would be the worst that could happen? Isn't that just what she'd been doing for the last week? That's *all* she'd been doing. Sometimes the greatest rewards came from the greatest risks.

"You *can't*, Tess. Promise me you won't—"

"I have to go." She interrupted Clara in the middle of her rant. "I have a lot of work to do if I'm going to get ready for the presentation tomorrow."

"Tess! You can't go through with it. Stick to the plan."

She could picture Clara, wherever she was, pacing back and forth, frantic because she was totally out of control of the situation.

"Don't worry, Clara." Tess smiled as the plan formulated in her head, suddenly feeling more confident and in control than she had since this whole mess started. "I have this whole thing under control. I promise." She disconnected the call before Clara could object again, tucked her phone away and headed back to the suite to get to work.

As it turned out, a project to get involved in was exactly what Tess needed to get her mind off Max. Except that everything to do with her project reminded her of her time spent with him. But she pushed those feelings aside and focused on the task at hand. With her dress swapped out for a t-shirt and shorts, her hair in a ponytail and a big mug of coffee to clear her head after the wine she'd had with dinner, Tess dove in.

The idea had come to her when Clara was telling her not to risk anything, but really, it had started to form much earlier. In fact, if she had to pinpoint the exact time when the light-bulb had gone off, it had been when her feet touched the wooden platform after that very first zip line in Breckenridge. In her entire life, Tess had never felt anything like the exhilaration of flying through the air, of landing on the other side knowing that not only had she survived it...she'd come completely alive. Everybody deserved to have that feeling. People needed to know that zip lines were not just for the thrill-seeking, adventurous at heart type of people. They were for *everybody*.

And that's exactly what her proposal was going to include.

Of course, she wasn't completely delusional. There were obstacles. And she'd have to address them. Not the least of which was the location where the zip line would have to be installed. It wasn't exactly easy access to the main Lodge. But maybe...an idea hit her like a flash. And it was just crazy enough to work. But she was going to need help.

And there was only one person who could help her.

Max wasn't going to lie; he was definitely surprised when he saw Tess's number show up on his cell phone. He'd tried to catch up to her, but he must have missed her by just a few minutes when he ran into Melissa, who informed him that Clara Clark would be giving her final report of recommendation the next morning. That had to have been Melissa's idea. There was no way Tess would suggest it.

Unless she had, in an effort to be finished with the project and to get away from Max faster.

That was also a very likely scenario. One that bothered him more than he cared to admit.

Regardless, he'd snatched up the phone and when she'd asked for his help, there was no way he was going to say no. Which was how he now found himself outside of her hotel suite, holding a box of pastries from Bruno, the head chef. It wasn't much in the way of a peace offering, but it was something and if they were going to be working late, they might need the sugar.

He knocked on the door and held his breath. As soon as she answered, the very first thing he was going to do was—

"Come in." Her voice called out from the other side of the door.

Okay. He'd have to modify his plan a little bit; that wasn't important, anyway. What *was* important was that Tess was still talking to him and he would get the chance to work everything out between them. Because he was confident that she was special and they would be able to get past this. He was sure of it.

"Tess." He walked into the room and stopped short when he saw her sitting on the living room floor, the couch pushed back, papers scattered everywhere, and a laptop on her lap. She looked beautiful with her hair all piled up on her head, pens sticking out of the mess, a coffee stain on her t-shirt and a general level of dishevelment that he would never have expected from her. It was a little insane how attracted to her he was at that moment. "I brought pastries," he said lamely and dropped them on the counter. "What's going on?"

"I need your help."

"I got that." He wandered over and picked up a piece of paper. It had a sketch of a log cabin on it. Another surprise. Although, he wasn't really sure what he expected to see. "Hey, before I help you with whatever you need help with, can we talk? I just really want to—"

"No." She sat up straight and looked him in the eye. "This isn't a social visit. I just really need your help, Max. I'm in way over my head, as I'm sure you already know."

"I don't think—"

"I just need your advice on a few things," she finished as if he hadn't spoken at all. "My best friend's business depends on it. And so does my future," she added quietly. "At least my immediate future."

He knew there was more to the story of why she was pretending to be Clara. That wasn't true. He knew there was *a lot* more to the story; he hadn't heard any of it so far, but he would be very interested in hearing it. *All* of it. But there'd be time for that later. Right now, he needed to focus. Max picked up a few papers and slid down on the floor across from her. "Okay," he said. "Tell me what you need. I'm here to help."

"Really?"

"I'm here. And I know you have a presentation to give tomorrow." He held up his hand in defense. "I ran into Melissa when I was out looking—on my way back from the village. She seemed a little...I don't even know what the word is."

"Predatory?"

He nodded. "That seems like a good way to describe it. But I'm not sure why she would be. She was the one who wanted me to hire you. Or Clara...or whatever."

"Right." If Tess caught any of his awkwardness, she ignored it and for that he was grateful. "Well, I can't be sure, but I get the feeling that she knows that maybe I'm not who I say I am and she made it really clear that honesty and integrity is the most important thing to her when it comes to business." She shook her head when he opened his mouth. "I know, okay? I don't need you to tell me that I haven't been very honest."

"I wasn't going to say that."

"And normally I wouldn't care that she seems to be setting me up for a fall, but my best friend's business is on the line here. She was trying to do me a favor, and I can't screw it up for her. She needs this. *I* need this. I have to do a good job with the recommendation but I can't use what Clara prepared. Not now that I know different things. I don't think it would be doing the project justice."

He was intrigued. No, Max was more than a little intrigued. This version of Tess was something he hadn't seen yet and he liked it. "Tell me about it."

She sat up straight and shoved the pen in her hand into the messy knot on the top of her head with the others. "Okay. Here's the thing." She handed him a piece of paper. "The original report Clara prepared is too safe. She had you adding a few overnight hikes, which you already do, some kayaking, and offering white water river rides."

Max scanned the paper. There were no surprises there. He'd been pretty certain her report would be tame. Safe. Boring. And that's exactly what it was. But it wasn't what he wanted to bring to the Lodge. Not even close. "And what do you propose?"

Her eyes danced with excitement. "This." She practically threw a notebook at him.

He read it through once and then again, slower. "Mountain climbing?"

She nodded. "Nothing like you're used to, I'm sure. But maybe a few basic instruction classes. And then you can set up kind of a permanent course that isn't too hard, but still makes the guests feel like they've really accomplished something. I heard that the outdoor activities manager, Bo, already does a bit of climbing, too. But it's not something you usually offer to guests."

"That's true. But with what you're suggesting, we can maybe make it more accessible. I like it." He nodded and continued reading. The overnight treks and kayak trips were all within what he expected, but it was the last item on the list that raised his eyebrows. "Zip line? Really?"

Tess's face lit up with a grin. "Absolutely. You have to offer a zip line and a treetop adventure trek. With lines, obstacles and…all of it. You have to."

He shook his head and put the notebook down. "I wish we could. But I just don't know how it would be possible."

Instead of looking defeated the way he'd expected, Tess came alive. She jumped to her feet and ran around the room, picking up pieces of paper. "It *is* possible. And that's where I come in."

She felt frantic, over the top, alive. Tess had never before felt so amazing with an idea that was all hers. Working as a payroll clerk, she'd never had an opportunity to use any creativity or create something, or really…do anything at all except type numbers in a box on the computer. But this, with all these ideas and papers and opportunities in front of her…*this* was something.

And judging by the look on Max's face, he thought so, too. He'd heard her pitch and was now looking over the papers with the sketches and projections she'd prepared. Every once in a while, he'd nod and smile. He hadn't stopped smiling since he sat down, but he still hadn't said anything.

She hadn't been totally sure about inviting him over; no, she'd been absolutely sure she didn't want him there. But it couldn't be about her feelings or about what made her comfortable or uncomfortable, because if that was the case, Max wouldn't be anywhere near her. No. It had to be about what was best for the presentation and Clara. She wouldn't let her friend down. Especially because she knew that the idea she had was gold. Clara didn't think so, but she didn't know what Tess knew. And she'd prove it.

"So?" She couldn't stand it any longer. "What do you think? Is it a terrible idea?"

"No." He flipped the papers around one more time before he stacked them neatly and looked up. "It's not a terrible idea at all. In fact, I think you might actually have something here."

"Really?"

He nodded. "Tell me again about the *hut*."

"Obviously, it wouldn't really be a *hut* but a building every bit as nice as the Lodge, just on a much smaller scale. It doesn't have to be called the Hut... I mean, I don't want people to think it isn't just as luxurious. But I thought it might be cute to market it as a smaller version of the Lodge."

"No. I like it."

A swell of pride surged up inside her, which was ridiculous because he was nothing to her. Well, he *should* be nothing to her. But she couldn't think about that now. She shook it off. She needed to focus. At least until after the presentation. "You really like it?"

"I do. But tell me how you plan on getting people to choose the Hut instead of the Lodge."

"That's the best part." Tess jumped up and grabbed a different piece of paper. She'd had the most fun coming up with the package ideas for this part of the plan. "I think people really do crave more adventure in their lives. I mean, it's easy to just wake up every day, show up to your regular life and *exist*. But I think we can show people how to really *live*. And we can do it in different ways. For example, a romance package doesn't have to mean only massages and candlelight bubble baths. I mean...those are good, but..." She blushed as the image of sharing a bubble bath with Max popped into her mind. "But adventure can be romantic, too." Tess refocused on the conversation. "Imagine spending a few days with your partner, working together to get through a treetop ropes course, experiencing the exhilaration of a zip line or the white water rapids. That would be incredible. I read somewhere that doing things with your partner that causes an adrenaline rush creates a stronger connection. Can't you picture it?"

"I absolutely can." He smiled at her in a way that made her stomach flip, but she had to ignore it.

Tess shifted gears. "And that's not all. We can do girlfriend getaways, team building packages, or even add-ons to the usual Lodge holiday. But because it's up a little farther from the Lodge, it's kind of like a separate getaway. A holiday within a holiday. I think we can really make this work."

He grinned and shook his head slightly.

"What?"

"I love that you keep saying 'we.'"

"Oh." She hadn't realized she was talking about it as if she'd be running it. Although, as she had worked out all the details, that's exactly what she'd been imagining. But that was getting ahead of herself. *Way* ahead of herself. First things first. "Do you think Melissa will go for it?"

Max shrugged. "I honestly don't know. I think she had a vision in her mind of *adventure-lite* activities. Something slightly riskier than a trail ride, but nothing that would cause actual danger. When she made me hire a consultant, I'm pretty sure her motive behind that was to get a report that basically said just that."

"That's what Clara wanted to give you."

"So this is all you?"

She nodded and held her breath.

"Then let's *make* her go for it."

Chapter Ten

BY THE TIME Max closed down the laptop after putting the finishing touches on the slideshow presentation, the sun had started to peek over the mountaintops. They'd worked through the night, but it hadn't felt like a chore because Tess's enthusiasm was contagious. It hadn't surprised him that Clara's recommendation was going to match the tame vision Melissa had. It had surprised him, however, that Tess had come up with an alternative that rivaled the image he himself had for the adventure program at the Lodge. No. It more than rivaled it; it far exceeded any ideas he'd come up with. It was perfect.

He glanced over to the end of the couch where she'd fallen asleep about thirty minutes earlier. There was no sense waking her when he just needed to finish a few things up. Besides, she'd need her rest if she was going to rock the presentation in a few hours. And he had no doubt she would. When someone was passionate about something as Tess was about this, it shone through in every way.

Working with her all night had been both amazing and torturous. All he'd wanted to do was pull her close for a kiss, but despite the amazing energy between them when it came to the business side of things, there was still an undercurrent of tension whenever they got too close. They'd bounced ideas off each other in what could only be described as a frenzy of brainstorming and then finally buckled down to creating the plan. Of course, they didn't have any projections on what it would cost to actually build the Hut or the zip line, but if the idea was received warmly, they could take that next step as well.

They.

If only there could be an actual *they*. The two of them would be perfect for this project. Together, Max knew they could make the Hut a reality. But, one thing at a time. First, they had to convince Melissa and then it would go to the Lodge owners, and then…feasibly they could be working on making the Hut and Castle Mountain Lodge the next best romantic adventure destination.

But first, coffee.

Max pulled a blanket up over Tess's slumbering body, resisted the urge to give her a kiss on the forehead and moved into the kitchen to see whether he could rummage something up for breakfast, or at the very least, make some coffee and order something from the restaurant. In the end, he chose the latter; he put coffee on to brew and ordered a hearty breakfast of eggs, toast, and fruit. They were going to need their energy.

While he waited for breakfast to show up, Max sprinted the short distance to the employee housing, grabbed a quick shower, put on his best shirt and ran back in time to meet room service at the door. He poured Tess a cup of coffee, put a plate of breakfast on a tray and as a last-minute touch, ran outside to grab a wild daisy, which he put on the tray.

"Good morning." Max put the tray down and rubbed Tess's shoulder. "Time to get up."

Her eyes fluttered and when Max caught the first glimpse of their beautiful blue color, his heart flipped a little. It was crazy to him that he felt so strongly about her after such a short time, but he did and just as soon as they finished up with what they had to do, he was going to make damn sure that she knew that.

"What smells so good?" She sat up and made a futile effort to smooth her hair back. Max was secretly glad she didn't succeed. Sure, he loved the way she usually looked, but there was something undeniably sexy about her first thing in the morning, with her hair all a mess and her clothes wrinkled.

Yes. Definitely sexy.

"I'd like to say I made it," he said. "But I ordered it from the restaurant. I made the coffee, though." He grinned and handed her the mug.

"My favorite part." She inhaled deeply and Max had to get up and move away from her, the attraction was so strong. "How long was I sleeping? What time is it?"

"Don't worry. It's only six thirty and really, you didn't sleep long. An hour, tops."

"The slides. Are they—"

"Done." He patted the laptop as he slid it into its case. "I put the finishing touches on them and everything is ready to go. All we need to do is get you showered and dressed, and…" He drifted off on that image. He shook his head and hoped she hadn't noticed. "We're all ready. But first you need to eat. I'll go ahead and get the screen set up in the meeting room and you can meet me there."

She nodded slowly and picked at the toast and egg. "Did you eat?"

"I was waiting for you." He couldn't keep the smile off his face as he went to retrieve his own plate from the kitchen and sat on the chair across from her to share another meal with this wonderful woman.

Tess couldn't remember the last time she'd been so nervous. Of course, as a payroll clerk, she'd never had the opportunity to do something so major. But her nerves were only overshadowed by one thing—excitement.

She had a good idea and she knew it. Plus, they'd worked hard. She glanced across the boardroom table at Max, who was still connecting wires and testing the projector. He'd been amazing and despite the drama that had gone down between them, he hadn't hesitated to come help her. They worked well together, even if she did have to resist the urge on more than one occasion to kiss him, or reach over and touch his hand. She was angry with him. She needed to remember that.

But for the life of her, she couldn't seem to remember why. Whatever reason she'd had the night before seemed so small now.

Really, really small.

"Are you ready?" Max was watching her with a smile. No doubt every single thing she was thinking showed on her face loud and clear.

She nodded. "I am. But there's only one more thing."

"What's that? I thought we'd covered everything."

All except one thing. Tess pulled her phone out of her bag. "I need to talk to Clara. She left like a dozen messages on my voicemail. She's freaking out and I can't blame her. After all, this is her company. She has a right to know what I'm doing. I just hope it's the right thing."

While she was talking, Max had circled the table and stood in front of her. He put a hand on her arm and squeezed. It was the first physical contact they'd had since their fight and her body responded immediately.

"It is the right thing, Tess. And I think Clara will see that, too."

"I hope so."

"She will. When she sees what you've put together here, she'll be so impressed with you. I know she will."

Tess wished she had half the optimism that Max seemed to have.

She nodded and turned to leave but Max pulled her back. "One more thing."

"What's that?"

"I think it's really important that we keep up the facade of you being Clara," he said. "I don't know Melissa all that well, but from what I do know and what you've told me, I think it's a good idea. We don't want her to be prejudiced on the idea before she even hears it."

Tess nodded again. It made sense. They were in a tricky situation and all she needed to do was to present her idea and leave. That's all Clara's company had been hired for. The fact that she'd imagined herself as part of the Hut and the process of bringing it all to fruition didn't matter. Her job was done when the presentation was finished. No matter what the outcome. Plain and simple. She just needed to keep her mouth shut. "You're right," she said after a moment. "But I still need to let Clara in on it. I emailed her the presentation a few minutes ago. She should be calling any—"

On cue, Tess's cell rang and Clara's face lit up the screen. She excused herself and took the call.

"Tess?"

"Hey. I'm really sorry, Clara. I know I should have answered your calls and called you back and—"

"Forget that now. I want to talk about what you emailed me."

Tess walked to the end of the hall where a window opened up to the courtyard. She held her breath and gazed out at the pines. "Look, Clara, I know it's not what we talked about and it's not at all what you had put together for the Lodge but there were some other factors and things that came to light—"

"I love it."

"I know you probably don't think it's...wait. What? You love it as in...you love the idea?"

"I do. I can honestly say that I never thought of the things you did and your presentation...well, it's top-notch, Tess. I'm really impressed."

"You are?"

"Don't sound so surprised."

She couldn't help it. Clara ran a successful company doing just what Tess had thrown together overnight. The fact that she loved it was not just surprising—it was awesome. "I'm really glad, Clara," Tess said. "You have to know that I would never do anything to put your business at risk and you know I appreciate everything you've done for me and—"

"Yeah, yeah." Her friend cut her off. "I know. It's all good. Now simmer down and no tears." Tess wiped at her eyes, which to her surprise had started to get watery. "You have an important presentation to do and I want to be there for all of it. Keep me on the line, okay?"

Tess didn't have time to object because at that moment she saw Melissa come down the hall. She put her phone on mute and hustled into the boardroom before the other woman got there.

After everyone was settled, and Tess had strategically positioned her phone, she stood and with shaking hands, took the little remote that would control the slideshow from Max.

"I'm very interested to see what you have for me today, Ms. Clark." Melissa looked even more impossibly put together than she had the day before. It was unfair how one woman could look so damn polished all the time with virtually no effort. It was also incredibly intimidating. A fact that Tess didn't focus on.

"I hope you'll be very impressed, Melissa." She turned her back to scoop up the papers with her information on it.

"I'm sure I will, Ms. Clark."

This time when Melissa said her name, she emphasized it in a way that made Tess's blood run cold. *She knew.* Tess glanced to the phone where she was sure Clara was listening and no doubt was coming to the same conclusion she just had. Melissa Kramer didn't strike her as a stupid woman and she also didn't come off as the type of woman to do or say things without a good reason for doing them. Tess glanced at Max, who was sending her warning signals. He wanted her to stay quiet. She took a deep breath, turned and made a decision.

"Before we begin, Melissa." Tess spoke and in that instant, Max knew he was not going to like the rest of the sentence. "There's something I need to tell you."

Oh no. No. No. He'd told her to keep quiet about the deception. It was one thing for her to come clean to him. But it would be an entirely different thing for her to own up to it to Melissa. She was definitely not going to be as understanding. *Not. Even. Close.*

"And what would that be?" Melissa leaned back in her chair and slowly crossed her long legs. She was an attractive woman, Max would have to be blind not to notice, but compared to Tess, Melissa's overly polished beauty didn't stand a chance. Not that he was there to compare the women. He most certainly was not. What he really needed to be doing was stopping the train wreck that was about to happen.

"I don't think we need to talk about that right now." He slapped the table in an effort to appear lighthearted. "In fact, let's get on with the presentation."

"No." Melissa held up her finger. "I'd like to hear what she has to say. Go ahead, Ms. Clark."

Tess took a quick breath and before he could try again, she was speaking.

"I know how important integrity in business is to you," Tess said and Max almost groaned out loud. "And that's why I need to tell you that my name is not Clara Clark; it's Tess Rogers. I'm a business partner and friend of Ms. Clark's and I was brought in at the very last minute to consult on this job. It was never our intention to deceive you or Mr. Grant." Max nodded for lack of anything better to do during Tess's confession. "Please know that I sincerely apologize for any misrepresentations or wrongdoing and I really do hope that it doesn't influence your opinion of the recommendation I'm about to give you."

Max held his breath, but beneath the surface, pride for the woman he was starting to fall in love with swelled. What she had just done had been unbelievably brave. He still didn't know the reason she'd pretended to be her friend, but he knew whatever it was, it had to be a good one and by coming clean just now, she put everything at risk.

"Did you know about this, Max?"

He nodded. "My suspicions were confirmed last night. But I need to—"

"I think we're done here." Melissa sat up with a snap and stood, dismissing them both.

"But you haven't heard my recommendation," Tess pleaded. "I've prepared—"

"I have no desire to hear whatever it is you have to say." Melissa smoothed her skirt. "From what I can tell, you aren't qualified in any way and you lied to me."

Tess's face fell and her shoulders slumped ever so slightly.

There was no way. They'd worked so hard on the idea. *Tess* had worked so hard. There was no way he was going to sit back and let Melissa dismiss her just for being honest.

"No!"

Both women turned and looked at him.

"Pardon me, Max?"

"No," he said again. "You need to hear the presentation, Melissa."

She shook her head. "I don't think so."

"You will regret it if you don't."

That caught her attention. She stopped. "And what makes you think that?"

"Because I've seen what Ms. Rogers has prepared and I think you'll be very impressed. The opportunity here for Castle Mountain Lodge is huge and I know you wouldn't want to miss out on that because of a misunderstanding."

"I hardly think it was a misunderstanding, Max."

"Well, maybe it was or maybe it wasn't," he said smoothly. "What's important now is you know who Tess is and that you listen to her very good ideas. I think if you don't, you'll be kicking yourself later."

Melissa looked down at the tabletop for a moment before she tapped her nails on the surface and looked up. "Five minutes," she said.

"That's all I'll need," Tess chimed in. And without missing a beat, she transitioned easily into the first slide.

Chapter Eleven

SHE COULD HARDLY BELIEVE it was over. What was more, Tess couldn't believe that Melissa had actually been impressed with what she'd said. She'd thought it was all dead in the water before she even began, but Max had really stepped up. If it hadn't been for him, there was no way Melissa would have sat and listened to what she had to say. More than that, she never would have actually liked what she presented.

In fact, she'd loved it. She agreed with Tess and Max that not only was the Hut a good idea, but it could possibly be the first thing of its kind in the area, making Castle Mountain Lodge even more of a destination. They could potentially capture a whole different market. Even a market that didn't know they wanted to experience the kind of adventure Castle Mountain could offer. The opportunity was there. And Melissa saw it.

After some handshakes, and even a verbal agreement with Clara on the phone that there would be no more misrepresentation between any of them, Melissa left to make some phone calls.

Her work was done.

"You did great," Clara said to her through the phone. "I am so proud of you, Tess."

She blushed a little, even though her friend couldn't see her. "It was nothing."

"It was everything," Clara insisted. "You not only saw an opportunity I totally overlooked, you put together a first-class presentation that some business executives couldn't even dream of doing. And you did it overnight."

"I didn't do it on my own." Tess looked over to where Max was disconnecting the projector and putting it back in the case. "I had a little help. No," she quickly corrected herself. "I had a lot of help."

"That was Max? The same Max you told me you were falling in love with?"

It wasn't a question that needed an answer, but she answered it anyway. "Yes."

"Do you still think you're falling in love?"

"It doesn't matter." But it did. It *really* did. But she couldn't tell Clara that. Especially not with Max right there in the room.

"That's bullshit and you know it." Tess could picture her friend pointing a finger in her face, getting ready for a lecture. "It does matter and you know how I know? Because you were willing to risk everything to tell him the truth. Everything. And I don't mean just you and the money you were getting from the deal. But you were willing to risk *us*." Clara's voice got low. "And you would never do that if it wasn't really important. And by really important, I mean…"

"I know what you mean, Clara. And you have to know I'd never do anything that I thought might hurt you. You know that, right?"

"Of course I know that!" Whatever emotion her friend had been feeling was gone, replaced by her characteristic optimism. "And I was a jerk for putting you in that position. But I'm glad

I did, because not only did it work out well for both of us, it *really* worked out well for you. I mean…Max."

Tess laughed at her friend. "I guess."

"No guessing. Get off the phone with me and go fix whatever it is that needs fixing between you two, because something tells me it's not all that bad. Then you can go and celebrate. And by celebrate, I mean—"

Tess hung up on her before she could get a graphic description on what celebrating really meant. She was pretty sure she could figure that out on her own.

"Is she happy?" Max used his head to gesture toward the cell phone Tess slipped back into her purse.

"She is," Tess said. "I think she was also pretty shocked that I could pull off something like that."

"I'm not."

Tess stopped and stared at him. "You're not?"

"No way." Max snapped the case shut and walked around the table until he stood in front of her. "I could see it in you right away. It takes a special kind of confidence to pull off something like that. Not everyone has that. But you do. I saw it the day you zip-lined. You're a lot stronger than you give yourself credit for."

"I don't know about—"

"You are." He put his hand on her cheek, and the sensations from his touch shot through her body until she wasn't entirely sure her feet would hold her up for much longer. "Tess, I need to apologize for everything. I never should have played any kind of game with you."

"No." She shook her head slightly and looked him straight in the eyes. "You have nothing to apologize for. It's me. I was the one who lied to you. And even though you had no reason to help me after everything I did, you were right there for me."

"I would do it again. And I did have a reason for helping you."

"What's that?"

His other hand rested on the opposite cheek so he was holding her firmly in place while his thumbs stroked gentle circles on her skin. "Because I think I'm falling in love with you, the woman I've come to know, the woman I'm just discovering, and the woman I've yet to learn about." And then he kissed her. It was the kiss she'd been waiting for from the first time they'd met because there were no secrets or lies between them. Just honesty and openness.

"Max?"

He pulled away so their noses were touching.

"I think I'm falling in love with you, too, and what I really want is to get to know you better and for you to get to know everything about me."

"I'd like that more than anything else. Except maybe this." He kissed her again and as Tess sank into the kiss, everything became crystal-clear.

Sometimes it wasn't about planning or preparation. Sometimes, the very greatest gifts in life and love were—accidental.

Chapter Twelve

September

Things had moved much faster than Max could have expected. As it turned out, Melissa liked the idea a whole lot more than she let on in the initial meeting, and not only did she call a handful of supplementary meetings, she went straight to the owners of the Lodge and made her recommendation, which to everyone's surprise, included having Tess head up further research plans and consult on the Hut. Despite Melissa's initial displeasure with Tess ultimately she respected her for coming clean and for producing such a comprehensive report.

For the last few months, Tess had been working from Colorado, while she tied up a few loose ends with her apartment, but today was the day she was scheduled to arrive at the Lodge. And Max couldn't help but think maybe it was for good.

They'd made the decision to put their relationship, if that's what you could call it, on hold while Tess was gone. They spent a lot of time on the phone and sending text messages, but it wasn't the same. But now that she was coming to stay for a while…well, anything was possible.

Max was up before the sun and had spent the last few hours making sure everything was ready. Not only for Tess's arrival, but also for the crew that was headed out to the site later that morning. Saying it was a big day would be a massive understatement. It was huge. He took another big gulp of coffee. Really huge. Because today was the day that they were finally going to start surveying and staking out the foundation for the Hut. And Tess would be right there with him.

He looked at his phone for the hundredth time. She hadn't called. Or texted. He knew her flight had arrived late the night before, and normally he would have gone to the city to greet her, but with the crews staying at the Lodge, he couldn't leave. Besides, Tess had said she would be up early and there by breakfast. Which should be any second.

But she hadn't called.

Max paced the lobby of the Lodge, which was mostly quiet at that time of day. He shouldn't be so nervous, but he couldn't help it. He hadn't seen her in months. Hadn't kissed her, hadn't—

There she was.

The taxicab pulled up at the sliding glass doors and before the doorman had made it to the door, Max knew: *Tess was inside that car.* He stopped, his feet frozen to the spot as the door opened and one denim-clad leg appeared. Followed by another. Followed by the beautiful brunette he'd been holding his breath for. She was gorgeous. And she wore the same pink plaid shirt she had the first day he'd brought her to the Lodge.

Without wasting another moment, Max strode outside and pulled her into a big hug. She felt so good in his arms. A perfect fit. As if there'd been something missing since he'd had to say good-bye. He buried his nose in her hair and inhaled. She smelled like…Tess. Like he never wanted to let go.

"Welcome back," he finally said when he released her from his arms. He wanted to kiss her so badly it was like a physical ache but he couldn't be sure how she'd react to kissing so publicly. Especially considering she was in a professional role at the Lodge now. So he waited. And it was the hardest thing he'd ever done.

"It's so good to be back," she said. "But it's a lot colder than it was at the beginning of summer." She wrapped her arms around her waist and he laughed.

"It's the mountains. It'll do that." He quickly ushered her inside so she wouldn't freeze. "We can get you all settled into your room after breakfast. The crew arrived last night and we're all organized to go out to the site. I printed out all the reports and I have all the safety equipment you'll need. But first I thought maybe we should—"

"Max?"

He turned and his heart skipped a beat when he saw the stern look on her face, her arms crossed over her chest. "Did I...what's wrong? Did I forget something?" He'd taken care of every detail. She'd been working so hard from afar that he wanted to be sure when she got to the Lodge she didn't have anything to worry about.

"Yes," she said. "You forgot this."

Tess threw herself into him and wrapped her arms around his neck. She pulled his mouth down to hers. She kissed him hard and there was no room for questioning exactly what he'd forgotten. His heart soared as their mouths explored each other. All of the heat, the passion, and the love from the last few months infused into that one moment and Max knew without a doubt that the two of them would be building more than just the Hut at Castle Mountain Lodge: they'd be building their future.

When finally they pulled apart and Max could look into

her beautiful blue eyes, he kissed her nose gently. "That's a mistake I'll never make again."

"Is that a promise?"

"Absolutely." He kissed her again. "Welcome home, Tess."

I hope you loved Accidental Gifts! The mountains really are the perfect place to fall in love! (Trust me... I know!)
There's a lot more love to be had at Castle Mountain Lodge. If you haven't fallen in love with the rest of the series, catch up with your favorite characters.
It's no secret that I love the mountains and if you enjoy them as much as I do, you'll want to check out the Timber Creek series that revolves around four best friends and their unique stories of second chances. These stories are heartwarming, full of love and of course a happy ever after!

You can read a sneak peak of When We Left right after this...

And if you want even more romance...click HERE for an exclusive FREE novella that isn't available anywhere else!

When We Left

Please enjoy an excerpt from *When We Left*, the first book in the Timber Creek Series.

When she looked back on it, she should have hung up on him. In fact, as soon as she saw his number come up on the screen, she should have tossed her cell phone out the window.

But she hadn't.

No. Of course not. A sucker for punishment, Cam Spears —*no*, strike that. Cam *Riley*—now was as good a time as any to go back to her maiden name—picked up her cell phone, steered her SUV with one hand and actually tried to have a conversation with her two-timing, philandering, no-good, son-of-a-bitch ex-husband. Well, he wasn't her ex yet. But he would be, soon. Hopefully *very* soon.

She'd spent way too much time turning the other way and pretending she didn't see what was going on right in front of her. Which was one affair after another.

"What do you want?" It wasn't the politest way to answer the phone, but there was no way Ryan actually deserved anything resembling manners from her anyway.

"I'm returning your call, Cam." He sighed in that way that might as well have said, "I'm far too important to deal with whatever it is you have to say."

Cam swallowed hard in a vain effort to control the wave of emotions that made her want to simultaneously scream obscenities and break down sobbing from frustration. "Right," she said as calmly as she could manage. After all, he was right. She *had* called him. "I wanted to talk to you about…" She glanced in the passenger seat at her teenage daughter. True to form, Morgan had her earbuds in, eyes closed and arms crossed. She was either sleeping or contemplating how much she hated her mother. Either way, she wasn't listening. "I wanted to talk to you about Morgan," she continued. "I'm hoping that a fresh start in a new town and a new school will be just what she needs to get her grades up and her attitude sorted out. And since no one knows her, she won't have to worry about the—"

"Right. Okay."

Cam tried to ignore the distracted tone in his voice.

"I've been really worried about her attitude lately. I mean, it's really gotten worse since the…"

"The separation?"

Cam swallowed hard and nodded. It wasn't that she was upset about the separation. Not in the way people probably expected her to be. But she was still having trouble wrapping her head around the fact that despite years of looking the other way, trying to make things work, and sacrificing her own needs and wants in favor of keeping their marriage together, it had all been for naught. The reality of what that actually meant for her and her daughter hadn't fully sunk in yet.

"Right," she said. "Anyway, I'm getting concerned that maybe she's—"

"I'm sure you can handle it, Cam."

Cam swerved slightly to the right before she corrected the steering wheel. "Pardon?"

The sigh again. "Come on, Cam. Honestly, why are you bothering me with this right now?"

"Bothering you?" She swallowed hard and struggled to keep her emotions in check. "Because she's your *daughter*, Ryan. We may be getting a divorce, but that doesn't change things with Morgan. We agreed to co-parent."

"About that…"

"About what exactly?"

"Well, things are kind of new between me and Chastity right now and with you moving out of town…Well, I think it might be easier if you could just handle things while Morgan is with you and when she's with me, I'll handle things. Ya know?"

There was no way he'd just said that. "Pardon?"

"It would be different if you stayed in town, Cam."

Stayed? There was no way she could have stayed in Portland. Not after what he'd done. Which was basically outing his affair and announcing his love child all over local television. As the co-anchors for the local evening news, Ryan and his new, much younger co-host, Chastity Newberry had been openly flirting on-air for months. Every time Cam mentioned it, Ryan brushed it off. But Cam wasn't stupid; she'd known about Ryan's indiscretions for years. He'd always been discreet about them and considering the love between them had died long before, Cam hadn't cared. Not really. Besides, he took good care of them, and there was no point stirring things up and blowing up their lives, just because they didn't love each other.

The *ostrich* approach had worked out well for Cam, too. At least until the weatherman, on the six o'clock news, with the entire greater Portland area watching—including everyone they knew—made an offhanded comment about the *happy new family to be*. There wasn't a sandbox deep enough for Cam to bury her head into after that.

She'd been humiliated in front of everyone. When Ryan came home, and told her he was in love with Chastity, and he wanted a divorce, Cam knew there was only one place for her to go.

"You know I couldn't stay." The words came out too soft, almost sad. She cleared her throat and tried again. "Besides," she said with a much stronger voice. "This isn't about me. It's about Morgan. I need you to—"

"You don't need anything from me. I'll always be there to love and support her and she knows that, but I can't get involved in your little parenting dramas right now. Besides, my lawyer doesn't think it's a good idea for us to be communicating. Not until the divorce is final."

Divorce. He made it sound so simple. So cold and clinical. As if almost fifteen years of marriage could be erased with a few pieces of paper. She didn't want to care, but she did because the truth was, even though she hadn't been in love with Ryan for a long time—maybe ever—there had still been a lot of positive in their relationship. A lot of good times, happy times and special memories. That couldn't just be wiped out with a few signatures on a piece of paper. *Could it?*

She ignored the feelings that tried to bubble up and tried to get back to the point. "Ryan, you're only going to see her once a month. That's hardly—"

"About that," he interrupted her. "I don't think that's very practical for me and with Morgan getting settled into a new school and everything—maybe if we did one weekend every two months instead?"

"What?"

"I'll have my lawyer contact yours."

The car jerked to the left. Cam quickly corrected it. "Wait." She struggled to wrap her mind around what he was saying. He didn't want to *see* their daughter? For everything she might have thought about Ryan as a husband, she never would have guessed that he'd be a bad father. "I don't—"

"Distracted driving is against the law, Mom."

Cam's head swung around to see Morgan staring at her, her lips pressed together, her eyes narrowed and attitude radiating from her pores. *She was awake? How much had she heard?*

"I'm not driving—"

"Yes, you are." Sighed with the drama that only a teenager was capable of.

"Cam, are you driving right now?"

"And there's a sign over there that says distracted driving is against the law in Washington." Morgan tapped her finger against the glass.

"I know it is, but…" She had bigger problems than holding a phone to her ear. *How much had Morgan heard her say?* "Morgan, you shouldn't have heard—"

"What?" Ryan barked in her ear. "Is she right there? Did Morgan hear you talking? Dammit, Cam. You should know better than—"

"Mom?"

"Cam. I can't believe you'd be so irresponsible."

"Me?" She slammed her hand down on the steering wheel. "*I* shouldn't be so irresponsible?" She yelled into the phone, no longer caring what Morgan overheard, at least for the moment. "Are you kidding me right now?"

"Mom?" Morgan glanced quickly behind her, but Cam barely noticed. "You should put your phone down."

With voices coming at her from all sides and her stupid emotions threatening to get completely out of control, Cam could hardly think and she definitely couldn't concentrate on the road, let alone on what anyone was actually saying. That's why when the siren sounded behind her, her first reaction was to slam on the brakes, followed by a loud, "Shit!" when she saw the flashing lights of the police car in her rearview mirror.

"Cam, what is—"

She ended the call, cut off Ryan's voice, and held the offending phone in her hand as though it were going to explode. She looked to Morgan for backup, but her daughter just shook her head and rolled her eyes.

Cam watched through the mirror as the officer stepped out of his car.

"Shit. Shit. Shit." Cam shook her head before she realized what she'd just said. As a positive example, she was doing a lousy job lately. To put it mildly. "Oh, Morgan. I'm sorry I swore. I shouldn't have used obscenities just because I was stressed out."

"Whatever." Morgan shrugged with indifference, but the satisfied smirk on her face gave her away. "I told you you should have put the phone down." She put her earbud back in and looked out the window.

———

There were a lot of things Officer Evan Anderson could ignore. Parking a little too close to the stop sign to run in and grab a coffee at Daisy's Diner. Sneaking up a few miles over the speed limit right at the edge of town where, in his opinion, fifteen miles was ridiculously slow anyway. Jaywalking across Main Street to say hello to a neighbor. These were all things Evan had no problem ignoring.

Driving erratically while talking on a cell phone was *not* one of those things. Distracted driving was dangerous and there was no way Evan was going to let it happen. Not in his town. Especially from someone with out-of-state plates.

With his lights flashing, he left his cruiser on the side of the road and made his way to the black SUV. Evan knew all the cars in Timber Creek, and most of the visiting family and friends too, and he certainly hadn't seen such a flashy-looking Expedition around town with Oregon plates before. Whoever it was who thought they could drive like an asshole in his town was about to get sorted out. He may not have respected Timber Creek the way he should have when he was still young and stupid, but that had changed. A lot. These days he took pride in protecting his home-town and making sure others respected it as much as he did.

He scratched down the license plate number before he made his way to the driver's side and rapped on the tinted window with the back of his hand. Evan began to talk the second the window moved down. "License and registration. Do you know why I pulled you over—"

The words died on his lips as the driver came into view. It was easy to see the woman behind the wheel was frazzled. Likely because she'd just been pulled over. But that's not what caught his attention, froze the words on his lips, and caused his heart to do a weird double flip in his chest. No, it was the familiar blonde hair—a little darker now—the profile of the nose he'd recognize anywhere because there had once been a time when he'd kissed the tip of it every single day, and then— when she turned to face him—her eyes.

Cam.

She was back? How was it even possible? He couldn't formulate a thought. Nothing coherent anyway and definitely nothing that would be remotely appropriate.

Fortunately, Cam spoke first. "Evan? Is that you?"

He blinked and swallowed hard, forcing himself to call on his army training to remain as stoic as possible and not let a damn thing show on his face. There was no doubt he was failing miserably, but it was better than nothing. "Cam?"

She smiled, but it didn't come close to reaching her eyes. "Yeah. It's been awhile. I can't believe you're a...well, you're a..."

"Cop?" He relaxed a little, seeing that she, too, was just as shocked. For sixteen years he'd dreamed about seeing her again. He'd fantasized about what it would be like to talk to her, to hold her, to—*no*. That clearly wasn't going to happen. It was still a traffic stop, after all.

Although writing a ticket was the furthest thing from his mind. "You didn't know?" He instantly regretted it. *Why should she know what he was doing now?* She'd left town right after graduation in search of what she used to call *a future*. He'd loved her more than life itself but even as an eighteen-year-old kid, he knew he was way too much of a screw-up to give her the future she deserved, so he'd let her go. Leaving him brokenhearted. And her…well, she'd moved on a long time ago. Without so much as a backward glance.

So why was she back?

Cam shook her head. "No. I didn't know. But I think it's great." There was that *not quite* smile again. The longing to see the warm smile he remembered so well hit him with a ferocity he didn't expect. "I'm really sorry if I was driving too fast, or…" She glanced down at her cell phone that sat incriminatingly in her lap. "Morgan told me not to, but I was just in the middle of a conversation, and I know it was wrong, but I wasn't thinking. I'm sorry. I mean, I know you'll have to give me a ticket and all, but—"

"Morgan?" For the first time, he noticed the teenager sitting in the passenger seat. He'd been so focused on Cam he hadn't seen past her.

"Hey." The girl waved sarcastically, no doubt very much aware of his preoccupation.

"My daughter. Morgan."

Daughter? She had a daughter. Of course she did. He knew she had a kid. But it was one thing to *know* she was happily married and had the life and family she'd always talked about. And a very different thing to *see* it with his own eyes. But he couldn't be surprised. Cam deserved it and it was all he ever wanted *for* her. But if that was true, why was there a flash of pain at the idea that it was somebody else who'd given it to her?

He smiled and nodded his head in the direction of the girl who looked as if she'd like to be anywhere but sitting in that car. "Nice to meet you, Morgan."

Cam's face turned red and she flapped her hands around a little, distracting him. "Here I am, not even back in town for five minutes and I'm already causing trouble."

"You're not causing trouble." He flipped his notebook closed and tucked it away in his pocket. There was no way he was going to write Cam a ticket. "What brings you back to town anyway?" He instantly regretted the question. Not because he didn't want to know. He did. Badly. Her parents moved to Arizona years ago, and as far as he knew, she hadn't been back since high school. *Why now?* That's what he really wanted to ask her, but when her mouth pressed into a thin line and she glanced down at her lap for just a second before she looked up again, her face now lined with a sadness and exhaustion that hadn't been there before, he regretted asking anything at all because the Cam he once knew slipped a little farther away.

"It was time," was all she said in response. "And we really should get going. If you wouldn't mind finishing up with my…"

"Oh." He shook his head and gave her a grin. "I'm going to let you off with a warning today. Keep your phone in your purse, okay?"

"You don't have to…I mean, you have to. Give me a ticket, I mean." She stumbled awkwardly over her words and glanced over at her daughter, who watched the entire scene with veiled disinterest. "I'm trying to teach Morgan consequences, and that means that I need to accept mine, too."

"I'm not giving you a ticket, Cam." He grinned and crossed his arms over his chest, in an effort to end the debate.

"You have to."

"No." He chuckled a little. He couldn't remember the last time anyone had begged him to give them a ticket. "I don't. But I really would like the opportunity to catch up with you while you're in town." Once again her face shifted and he regretted his choice of words. *Dammit.* She probably thought he was letting her off the hook in exchange for a date.

"I'm not sure that's a good idea, Evan." Her voice was tight. "But if you're really not going to give me a ticket, I should get going."

"I'm not." He took a step back from the SUV. "It really was nice seeing you, Cam."

In response, she put her window up, pulled away, and drove down the road. Just as she had all those years ago. Leaving Evan standing in the dust, wondering what the hell had just happened.

Evan. He was here. Of course he was here. It was his town. Why wouldn't he be there? Why shouldn't he?

Because he left.

He'd left her more than sixteen years ago.

Cam's head hurt with the memories that hit her with a tsunami force the second she saw those familiar eyes. She reached up and rubbed the bridge of her nose. She didn't have time for a headache. She didn't have time for anything. Especially thinking about Evan and a past that couldn't be changed.

"Who was that guy?"

Morgan. She needed to remember that just because Morgan stayed largely quiet didn't mean she didn't notice anything. In fact, it was quite the opposite.

"Who?" She tried to keep her voice light and unaffected, but her daughter clearly wasn't buying it.

"Who do you think?" Morgan rolled her eyes. "The only guy we've seen in the last few hours who wasn't pumping gas. The cop, Mom. Who is he? You know him."

She shook her head because the truth was she didn't know him. Not anymore.

"I used to," she answered honestly. "But that was a long time ago." A really long time ago and she didn't have time to consider what Evan's presence in Timber Creek would mean to her. Of course she'd known logically that he *could* be here, but Christy Thomas, her one friend who still lived in town, had never mentioned him. Likely out of concern for Cam and an unspoken understanding that Cam didn't want to know. Not really. It wouldn't do any good to revisit the past.

"I'm sure we'll run into lots of people I used to know," she said to Morgan, trying to keep her tone light and fun. Maybe if she made her return to her hometown an adventure, her daughter would buy in. It was a long shot, but it couldn't hurt to try. Lord knew she'd tried everything else to get Morgan engaged in life. She'd been chalking Morgan's behavior up to the typical teenage type of drama, but now with the added *bonus* of dealing with a public family breakdown on top of everything else, she almost couldn't blame her daughter for acting out.

Almost.

Morgan hadn't said much about her dad or the new baby, or really any of it. Whenever Cam tried to bring it up, she just clammed up. Cam was running out of ideas on how to deal with it but a fresh start could only help.

"Whatever." Morgan rolled her eyes and put her earbuds back in.

Cam tried not to sigh. There was no point starting something with her. They'd be out of the car soon enough and maybe it was best if Cam was left alone in her own thoughts and memories for the drive through town. It was always her favorite part about coming home when she was a little girl. Her parents would take her on countless trips throughout the United States, to exotic beaches, the castles of Europe, or even on her tenth birthday, to Disney World. But despite all her travels, Cam's favorite part of traveling had always been coming home. Turning the bend to see the log sign proclaiming, "Timber Creek, Home of the Timber Times Festival," had meant she was only minutes away from being in her room, sleeping in her own bed and seeing all her best friends: Christy, Drew, and Amber.

It's not that she hadn't liked traveling; she just never loved it the way her parents had. Sure, she appreciated having the opportunity to see the world and experience the things she had, but there was something about home that she couldn't find anywhere else.

Just as it did all those years ago, a familiar sense of peace came over her as she drove down Main Street, which was completely the same yet totally different all at the same time. It had taken her sixteen years, and the circumstances were less than ideal, but she was finally home.

She glanced at Morgan, who stared out the window, her lips pressed into a thin line. No doubt she'd complain about the lack of malls, the tiny streets, the small classrooms, and pretty much everything else about Timber Creek that was in direct opposition to Portland. But that was okay. Cam could handle it because whether Morgan knew it or not, Timber Creek was going to heal them. It had to, because Cam was completely out of options.

There'd be plenty of time later to show Morgan the sights of Timber Creek. Not that it would take long, but for now, all Cam wanted to do was get settled so she could start thinking about her next step. A step that would need to include a job and getting Morgan enrolled in school as soon as possible. The therapist she'd sent Morgan to before Ryan cut her benefits off had suggested building a strong, structured routine for Morgan as soon as possible. If she knew there was stability in her life, she'd be less likely to act out.

Stability. Ha. The very word made Cam want to laugh and then cry. There was definitely not a lot of stability to be found, but she'd do what she could. They both needed it.

She pulled the SUV up in front of Junky's Auto Shop, looked up and let her eyes take in the grungy windows of the apartment over the shop with a faded For Rent sign in the window.

When Cam had called Christy to tell her she was going to be returning to town, she was adamant about getting her own place, something "stable" and "structured" for Morgan. When her friend finally stopped trying to convince her to stay with her and her husband Mark, she told her about Junky's apartment and because Christy was able to do some sweet talking, Cam got it at a reduced rate. Although, now that she was looking at it, she couldn't help but think it had something to do with the fact that the place likely hadn't seen a broom or a rag in years. *If ever.* And that was only what she could ascertain from the outside.

"Why are we here?" Morgan stared at her. "Is the car broken now?"

There was nothing to do but put a brave face on. "Nope," Cam said with as much forced cheerfulness as she could muster, which really wasn't much. "This is our new home."

Morgan's face screwed up in disgust. "You can't be serious. An auto shop?"

"No. The apartment above it." She pushed the button to cut off the engine, and turned to gather up her purse. The sight of a police cruiser in her rearview mirror caught her eye, but by the time she turned around to confirm, it was gone. *Evan.* No doubt he was just making sure she was getting to wherever she was going safely.

Because he still cares about you.

No.

She had no time for Evan or thoughts of Evan or anything at all to do with the past. That's not why she came home. This time, the only thing Timber Creek was going to give her was her future.

"I'm sure it's fantastic, Morgan." Cam forced herself to switch gears. Hopefully the apartment wasn't *too* bad. Even if it was, it wasn't anything a bucket of soapy water and maybe a can of paint couldn't fix. Nothing was going to bring Cam down, or deter her from starting fresh. Nothing.

"Whatever." Morgan slid down in her seat, arms crossed firmly over her chest.

"Come on, Morgan." She turned in the seat and placed her hand on Morgan's arm. To her surprise, her daughter didn't shrug her off. It was such a small thing, but when it came to dealing with Morgan lately, Cam would take whatever victories she could get, no matter how small. "I know it's not ideal and it's a little different than what we're used to."

"A *little?*"

"Okay, a lot." Up until a few days ago, they'd been living in the only house Morgan had ever known, a three-thousand-square foot mansion on the water in one of Portland's most prestigious neighborhoods. One of the perks of being married to the local news anchor. One of the only perks. Cam swallowed hard against the bile in her throat. It was a beautiful house, and she'd taken a lot of pride in making it a home over the years, but it would never be home again. Not anymore.

There was no point dwelling on things. She needed to focus. Besides, Morgan didn't deserve to be drawn into any more drama than she already had been. *Stable and secure.* That's what she needed to remember.

"Look, Morgan." She squeezed her daughter's arm gently. "I know it's not much, and it's not permanent, but it will be ours and we might actually have a lot of fun fixing it up just the way we want. We can paint it bright colors and maybe get some funky pillows and things. It'll be fun. Promise me you'll at least give it a chance."

She stared into her daughter's heavily eye-lined eyes, and hoped upon hope that something she said might be getting through to her. For a moment, she thought Morgan would close up again and shut her out, but then she nodded. "Okay."

It wasn't much, but it was all Cam needed. "Okay. Let's go find Junky." Her face split into a smile she definitely didn't feel, and she jumped out of the car before Morgan could change her mind again.

Cam definitely has her hands full. Is a second chance with Evan really in the cards when she has so much going on? Find out what happens and read the rest of When We Left now!

About the Author

Elena Aitken is a USA Today Bestselling Author of more than forty romance and women's fiction novels. The mother of 'grown up' twins, Elena now lives with her very own mountain man in the heart of the very mountains she writes about. She can often be found with her toes in the lake and a glass of wine in her hand, dreaming up her next book and working on her own happily ever after.

To learn more about Elena:
www.elenaaitken.com
elena@elenaaitken.com

www.ingramcontent.com/pod-product-compliance
Lightning Source LLC
Chambersburg PA
CBHW022032170626
46808CB00003B/1166